D E A T H

Peter Goldsworthy was born in Minlaton, South Australia, in 1951. He grew up in various country towns, finishing his schooling in Darwin. Since graduating in medicine from the University of Adelaide, he has devoted his time equally to medicine and writing. He is married to a fellow graduate and they have three children.

Peter Goldsworthy has published three collections of poetry, including *This Goes With That: Selected Poems 1970–1990,* and four collections of short fiction. He is the author of three novels: *Maestro, Honk If You Are Jesus* and *Wish*, his most recent work. He has won numerous awards including the Commonwealth Poetry Prize and an Australian Bicentennial Literary Award.

Also by
Peter Goldsworthy

Poetry

Readings from Ecclesiastes
This Goes With This
This Goes With That: Selected Poems, 1970–1990

Short Fiction

Archipelagoes
Zooing
Bleak Rooms
Little Deaths

Novels

Maestro
Magpie (jointly with Brian Matthews)
Honk If You Are Jesus
Wish

PETER
GOLDSWORTHY

DEATHS

Angus&Robertson
An imprint of HarperCollins*Publishers*

Angus&Robertson
An imprint of HarperCollins*Publishers,* Australia

First published in Australia in 1993
Reprinted 1993, 1995
This edition 1995
Reprinted 1996
by HarperCollins*Publishers* Pty Limited
ACN 009 913 517
A member of the HarperCollins*Publishers* (Australia) Pty Limited Group

HarperCollins*Publishers*
25 Ryde Road, Pymble, Sydney, NSW 2073, Australia
31 View Road, Glenfield, Auckland 10, New Zealand
77-85 Fulham Palace Road, London W6 8JB, United Kingdom
Hazelton Lanes, 55 Avenue Road, Suite 2900, Toronto, Ontario M5R 3L2
and 1995 Markham Road, Scarborough, Ontario M1B 5M8, Canada
10 East 53rd Street, New York NY 10032, USA

National Library of Australia Cataloguing-in-Publication data:

Goldsworthy, Peter, 1951–
Little deaths.
ISBN 0 207 18930 7.
I. Title.
A823.3

Typeset in 11pt Bembo
Cover photograph: Jody Dole/The Image Bank
Printed in Australia by Australian Print Group

9 8 7 6 5 4 3   96 97 98 99

CONTENTS

ACKNOWLEDGMENTS

Several of these stories have previously been published.
My thanks to *The Adelaide Review*, *The Sydney Review*,
Paris Transcontinental, *Quadrant* and the annual
Winters' Tales anthology (New Series Eight) for permission
to reprint. Several have been broadcast by the BBC.
'The List of All Answers' was rescued from the clutches of an earlier,
more embarrassing book, *Zooing*, and revised slightly.

Peter Goldsworthy

The
CAR KEYS

1

Later, Barbara remembered a platitude she had read some-where: an orgasm was a kind of death, a little death.

A death-*throe*.

At the time, lost in her own death-throes — not-so-little — she failed to comprehend Luke's strange, exaggerated moaning. He was outside the high walls of her own pleasure; she half heard him, but thought it — *half* thought it — some sort of joke. From the start there had been moments of irreverence, of clowning, in their relationship: an antidote perhaps to the illicit lust, extremely serious, that fuelled it.

His noisy groaning seemed a self-parody at first, a cartoon-come, but the sudden chill in his skin, the cold, clammy sweat, shocked her. She was instantly alert, dragged back from a charged erotic world, where pain sometimes meant its opposite, into the real world, where pain meant nothing but pain.

'Luke? What's the matter? Is something the matter?'

She realised — an even sharper instant of terror — that he couldn't answer. He no longer had the breath to inflate the words; he stared up at her from the floor with mute horror. He was in agony.

'Oh, shit!' she screamed, and lifted herself free from him, and ran to the phone.

She scrabbled, fingers trembling, through the teledex for the emergency number, stammered her address into the phone. The operator wanted more information; she was too agitated to answer, straining at the receiver, trying to glimpse her lover lying in the hall, wanting to get back to him.

'What does it *matter* how old he is, for Christ's sake?' she screamed. 'Just *get* here!'

What next? She sat cradling his head, helpless, waiting for the ambulance. He sucked laboriously at the air, dragging the stuff into his lungs as if it were treacle. His limbs flailed weakly — some kind of semaphore, perhaps, which she couldn't read. They were both still naked, their clothes scattered over the length of the hall. He had rung earlier from his office, demanding to see her, to *touch* her, unable, he claimed, to wait for their weekly meeting; she had opened the front door to him a few minutes later, and allowed him, for the first time, into the sanctuary of her own house. Her *husband's* house. But not into her bed — not into the bed she shared with her husband: that still remained as a last, absurd, scruple. Guilt was inescapable, but perhaps there were degrees of guilt: guilts that could be lived with, or tolerated, barely.

She had pushed him down onto the carpet in the bedroom doorway. His feet were in the hall, his head and shoulders in the bedroom. She had permitted him halfway into her life, halfway into her privacy, but no further.

'Please, Luke,' she whispered. '*Please* don't die.'

The wailing of the approaching ambulance shocked some sort of sense, or self-awareness, into her brain. She slipped a pillow beneath his head, pulled on a sweater and jeans; then tried, urging him to help, to clothe him. His movements were still ineffectual, even pointless. She forced his jocks on, despite his dripping, half-tumescent state. Tears blurred her eyes, her movements were panicky and confused. She half pulled, half pushed his trousers on, a little roughly; he seemed to shift his weight to help automatically, a reflex movement. There was no time for his shirt: the siren died in the street outside; she shouted in his ear: 'I won't be long, Luke. The ambulance ....'

He couldn't answer. His eyes had glazed over; his breathing, it seemed, had almost stopped. She touched his white face; it felt as cold as stone. An Easter Island face, she had once told him, jokily, tracing with her finger the long nose and narrow crown. It was closer now to those impassive stone statues than it had ever been.

She rose, jerked open the front door and ran to the gate: 'Help! Please! I think it's a heart attack.'

The ambulance was crawling along the kerb, its driver — a young woman, almost a girl — scanning house numbers. She spotted Barbara waving frantically, and slewed the vehicle into the gutter; an older, uniformed woman jumped out from the passenger side and ran towards the house, carrying a large box and canister of oxygen.

'Where is he?'

'This way. Quickly.'

The older woman knelt at Luke's side, felt briefly for a pulse in his neck, then turned and spoke calmly to her younger colleague, the driver, who was lugging a collapsible stretcher down the hall.

'It's an arrest, Emma.'

She rolled Luke flat onto his back, pressed a facemask to his pale, sweaty face, and began squeezing an air-bag, rhythmically. The younger woman, Emma, dropped her stretcher and began pressing the heels of her palms into his chest, up and down, a slightly faster rhythm.

Barbara watched: helpless, distraught.

'We've got a pulse,' the older woman announced, and turned to Barbara. 'Here, you squeeze this.'

'Me? But I *can't*. I mean, I don't know *how* ...'

'Like this.'

The voice was firm, calm, controlled. The bag was pushed into Barbara's right hand, her left was clamped over the facemask and chin. She held tightly with one hand, squeezed with the other.

'A little slower. Perfect. Listen — is your husband on any medication?'

'Uh — no. I don't think so.'

The younger woman glanced up at her sharply: 'You don't *think* so?'

'He's not my husband.'

This did not seem adequate; she hurried on: 'Luke is ... um ... a close friend of my husband.'

Was there anything more stupid she could have said? Luke had never *met* her husband. The phrase seemed to leap from her mouth with its eyes closed, a compounding of guilt.

The younger woman watched her for a moment — *stared* at her, openly, curiously — then turned away, still pressing Luke's chest. The older, unperturbed, was pushing a needle into the crook of his elbow. Her manner was been-there-done-that, unshockable.

'You want to ride in the ambulance?' she offered.

Barbara hesitated. Their professional calm was infectious, she seemed able to think more clearly.

'I'll follow in the car. I should make some phone calls first.'

2

Who to call? First instincts said Gerry, her husband, to prepare the ground, fit together the ribs of a plausible story. She rebuked herself: Luke's kin had the prior claim, surely. But where were they? *Who* were they? She realised suddenly how little she knew of him. They had met only a few weeks before: swapping Royal Family jokes across a magazine rack in a newsagent, followed by a cappuccino in a café next door, the jokey laughter suddenly more nervous, at least on her side. She was aware that merely by accepting his invitation to coffee she had crossed a new boundary.

This much he had told her: he was a solicitor, but business was slow, he was largely unemployed. His self-deprecating manner, however well-practised, charmed her. She first visited his apartment a few days later — heart pounding — unable to refuse his phone demands any longer.

He had seldom spoken of his ex-wife, although occasionally boasted of his small son. Framed portraits of a single smiling infant abounded in an otherwise minimally decorated bachelor pad.

He silenced her when she attempted to speak of her own children.

'I don't even want to know their names,' he said. 'That's your other life. Different compartment. It has nothing to do with this.'

Even as they stripped at that first assignation he had been quick to establish these ground rules. Too quick, she thought afterwards. Too ... cold-blooded.

'We won't do this again,' she had assured him, pulling on her clothes, overcome with regret, wanting only to be home and safe as quickly as possible. 'Not ever. It's not right.'

He sat naked in bed, propped on pillows, watching her dress: an impassive Easter Island head.

'It might not be right,' he said, 'but it can be made civilised.'

'What do you mean?'

'There are ways of doing these things, Barbara.'

'Not for me there aren't. Never again.'

Her resolve lasted a week. She was drawn back to him more by confusion than by desire: by a need to settle her disturbed state of mind, one way or another. Also by the need to talk about it — there was no one else she could talk with. She still felt uneasy, afterwards — but felt also, absurdly, that it would be, well, *rude* to rush off again so quickly.

'There are rules for war,' he murmured into her ear as they lay together. 'A Geneva convention. War is wrong — but it happens. It will always happen. We can only attempt to limit the damage.'

For the first time she felt comfortable enough to tease him: 'You sound like a lawyer.'

'Perhaps there are rules for adultery,' he suggested. 'Laws of adultery.'

Her pulse flared at the sound of the word. Adultery. A small thrill of torment passed through her each time she heard it. Or even, in the coming days, read it: there suddenly seemed any number of adultery stories in the newspaper; the word kept finding her eye, jumping off the pages as if set in bold type, as if embossed.

She had announced her own laws the following week. She loved her husband. She would never leave him. He must never, ever know.

Her conviction on this point seemed, oddly, to reassure her lover: a safety net had been stretched beneath their difficult trapeze act, protecting him, perhaps, as much as her.

'He won't *want* to know,' he reassured her.

She wasn't convinced: 'I read somewhere that they always know. Within a few hours. They read the signals.'

'Wives know,' he told her. 'Men aren't so ... sensitive.'

Relieved, she found this easy to accept: 'Gerry *doesn't* notice small things. He's so bound up in his work. He ...'

Luke pressed his fingertips against her lips: 'I don't even want to hear his name.'

'You're right,' she said. 'It's not fair. To him.'

She sensed that Luke had been here before, more times than once, that he was allowing her to discover these excuses, these rationalisations: the rules and procedures, if such things were possible, of adultery. The etiquette of adultery. At times his answers to her worries came too easily, too glibly: a frictionless gear change. But she was grateful even for this. At other times, more subtly, he deflected her questions back at her, allowing her to discover the answers that he only hinted at.

He had pursued her relentlessly from their first meeting; but somehow, now, after talking it through — gnawing together at the same bone, obsessively — it had come to seem an equal responsibility.

'What if I talk in my sleep?' she asked him once.

'*Do* you talk in your sleep?'

'It might burst out of me. I've never lied to him.'

He seemed more pensive than usual. His answer took a long time to emerge: 'The worst thing you can do is make a confession.'

'You sound as if you're talking from experience.'

He averted his face. It was the nearest he had come to autobiography, to providing clues to the fate of his own marriage.

As the ambulance siren faded into the general noise horizon of morning traffic, Barbara realised that she had never once heard his ex-wife's name.

3

She tugged the *Yellow Pages* from a shelf and searched under 'Solicitors' for his work number. She had rung him several times at his office — a small suburban shop front — but had not yet committed the number to memory. No, had *refused* to commit the number to memory: to memorise such details was to grant the affair a permanency that she still resisted.

'Is that Luke Pascoe's office?'

A butter-voiced secretary assured her that Mr Pascoe was 'out with a client'.

'He's in hospital,' Barbara interposed, bluntly, 'with a suspected heart attack.'

The voice at the far end of the line was suddenly higher-pitched and panicky: 'But he can't be! He was here — just an hour ago.'

'I'm sorry. I wondered — it looks serious. If you could contact his family ... He's at the Queen Adelaide.'

'Are you a nurse?'

Barbara was given no opportunity to lie as the voice raced on, terrified, tearful: 'Give him my love. Please. Tell him Sandra sends her love. I'll be right there.'

As she hung up Barbara realised, stunned, that she had opened at least one bulkhead, inadvertently — a hatch that led into another of Luke's compartments: a dark crawl space she had no desire to enter.

She gathered her purse and car keys, stepped out of the house, locked the front door. Preoccupied, she had climbed into her car, started the engine, and begun reversing before turning to check the drive.

Luke's car — a red sports coupé, a car that suddenly looked more like a cliché than a car — was parked behind hers, blocking her exit.

She braked suddenly, inches from his front fender. She climbed out and peered into the coupé. The doors were locked, the ignition empty. With a sinking feeling she re-entered the house, and spent some minutes searching the hall and bedroom carpet on hands and knees for his key-ring. The search was as futile as she had dreaded: the keys were surely in his pocket, speeding towards hospital.

She rang a taxi with trembling fingers, then waited, fidgeting, restless, outside in the street. Luke's car glinted in the sun, incandescent red, drawing the entire world's attention to itself: Exhibit A. Her predicament overwhelmed her; the desire she had felt for him, the frightened thrill of those secret visits, was suddenly beyond her comprehension. What *had* she been doing? That immovable object, parked in her drive, filled her thoughts to the exclusion of all else — even her worry over whether Luke was still alive.

She had two hours, perhaps three, before Gerry arrived home from work. A taxi turned the corner. She stepped down into the road and waved both her arms above her head, desperately.

4

'Are you his wife?'

'No, just a friend. How is he?'

The nursing sister — a young, thin man, his hair gripped tightly in a ponytail — watched from behind a desk.

He half rose and gestured to a chair: 'Perhaps you'd better sit down.'

Barbara remained standing in the door of the office, already knowing: those words were a formula, an explanation in themselves; they had nothing to do with the act of sitting.

He shrugged, and sat again himself: 'He died a few minutes ago. I'm very sorry.'

'Could I see him?'

He glanced down, pretending to scan some notes on his desk: 'We need to contact his family first. Next-of-kin. Perhaps you can help us trace them?'

'No. I'm sorry ... But his secretary will be here soon. Sandra somebody. I'm sure she can help.'

Her legs felt weak. She finally sat on the offered chair; hating herself for what she had to do, for the selfish premeditation of it: a further betrayal. And yet it seemed a lesser betrayal: her first loyalty now was to the living.

'Look, um, Sister. I have a small problem. I think my car keys are in his pocket.'

'I can look,' he offered, and rose, and slipped past her through the door. The office was glass partitioned, she watched him disappear behind the curtain of a nearby cubicle, allowing her no glimpse of whatever that curtain concealed. He re-emerged almost immediately, carrying a small cardboard box: a labelled shoebox: PASCOE, LUCAS.

'His personal effects.'

He eased free the thick rubber band which bound the box and lifted the lid. It contained a watch, a black leather wallet, a miscellany of coins — and the missing keys, a key-ring attached to a plastic chequered flag, poignantly jaunty.

Barbara reached across the desk, but the nurse slid the box out of reach. His tone was apologetic but firm: 'I'm sorry, I should have explained. Personal effects are the property of the coroner's office. We can't release them. Not yet.'

Her hand stayed frozen above the desk, as stiff as the arm of a gramophone: 'But I have to move the car.'

He watched her intently: he seemed to be examining her. She realised, suddenly, that he had been in this position before.

'Okay,' she confessed. 'It's *his* car. But it's blocking *my* drive.'

'I'm very sorry,' he said. 'Really. If it was up to me ...' He shrugged. 'But there are procedures we have to follow — by law. Until the coroner releases the body.'

She could feel the panic growing in her: 'When will that be?'

'After the autopsy. In fact, you might be able to help, Ms ...?'

'Mrs Browning.'

'Mrs Browning. I gather you were present when he first became ill.'

She sat, saying nothing, admitting nothing.

'Perhaps if you could describe the symptoms ...'

A crazy thought crossed her mind: to strike some sort of deal. A swap.

'I just want to move a car,' she said.

'Mrs Browning — please. I *can't* help. But if you were a witness I think the doctor would like a word with you.'

'I wasn't there. I don't know anything. *Please* give me the keys.'

'Perhaps you could call a locksmith.'

'That might take hours! I need to shift it *now*.'

Tears welled in Barbara's eyes, but they were not tears of grief — whatever grief she felt had been deferred, under pressure of greater, more selfish emotions. What was she to do? What were the rules, the procedures? What subsection of Luke's absurd Geneva Convention dealt with this? She felt an overpowering, irrational urge to enter the curtained cubicle and demand answers from the dead body, the dead lawyer who was filed there, discreetly out of sight. *What now? What do I do now? Tell me the precedents.*

On the other side of the desk the nurse fitted the cardboard lid carefully over the shoebox of personal effects, stretched the thick rubber band about both, and released it with a soft snap.

Rage overwhelmed Barbara: rage at this man who had died in her house, on her carpet, who had thoughtlessly, carelessly, left his car blocking her drive. She reached across the desk and grabbed the shoebox from the nurse's hands with such force that he could only watch, stunned. She jerked off the lid, and extracted the keys.

'I'll return these later,' she said.

And she rose and walked rapidly from the cubicle and down

the corridor, those stolen keys grasped tightly in her hand, the nursing sister still sitting behind his desk, watching her leave, paralysed by surprise.

The Death of
DAFFY DUCK

The two couples had eaten together once a month since their university days; eaten their way through the menus of most of the decent restaurants in the city, and more than a few of the indecent. At times others shared their table — other couples, the odd 'confirmed bachelor' friend or visiting relative — but the booking was usually a Table For Four.

Things had gone well over the years for the four, professionally. Terry Hicks had established himself as one of the younger, and braver, bone surgeons in the city; his wife Mary — Mary Barratt, one of the first of her generation to keep her maiden name — taught architecture at the Institute. Scott and Jenny Greaves were both lawyers: Scott a barrister with the Crown Law Department, Jenny a private solicitor, dealing mainly with Family Law briefs.

Neither couple had yet produced children, although the time for final decisions was fast approaching. The women were now mid-thirties, and at times, especially late at night — alone with themselves, isolated by insomnia from the snug, sleeping world that surrounded them — both felt the odd prickle of anxiety. Their various mothers and fathers and mothers-in-law had long ago dropped the subject — on pain of death — but both women retained a half-conscious understanding that yes, they *would* one day have children, even if they denied the wish in public.

Meanwhile, there was still fun to be had, childless freedom to enjoy. The monthly dinners were riotous affairs; money was thrown about as loosely as talk, course followed course, imported liqueurs followed imported wines, the tips at the end of the night were uniformly big irrespective of service. Mary (the architect) had a penchant for desserts. Her meal often consisted of nothing but an entrée, followed by three different rich desserts; yet somehow she maintained the trimmest figure. Too trim, her friend Jenny privately thought, although in public Jenny always expressed mock chagrin at the quantities of food Mary permitted herself. In their schooldays together Jenny had been the ugly one, tagging along in Mary's wake; now she felt more equal, was *made* to feel more equal, even, or especially, by the men. Clothes of most kinds still hung best on Mary but in a swimming pool, or naked before a mirror, Jenny was fully aware of who was more womanly in shape and volume. She was careful to keep her shape that way, but no more, by sticking to small picky seafood portions, salads, fruit platters.

It was usually Jenny's insistence that led to the choice of restaurant: nouvelle cuisine, northern Chinese, southern Thai, once even a vegetarian place.

The bill was rotated between the couples, although if someone forgot their wallet or purse, or paid out of turn, no one worried — money seemed plentiful, generosity was a virtue that all four could easily afford.

At the birthday dinners — four a year — extravagant gifts changed hands: imported perfumes, cameras, wines, electronic toys. Spending on *anything*, for its own sake, was a form of generosity, Scott (Deputy Crown Prosecutor at thirty-five) proclaimed on one such occasion. Small, wiry, quick with his tongue, he liked to harangue his friends as if they were jurors. There was nothing *wrong* with conspicuous consumption, he pronounced, as long as the money was spent quickly enough.

'The *velocity* of money is what matters, not the amount. You have to keep the money moving. If everyone spends quickly enough, everyone can take turns being a millionaire.'

'Briefly,' his wife quibbled.

'Does that matter? You still get to spend the money.'

There had been occasional hiccups in the relationship; in particular one upper-case Scene involving a smashed glass between the men. Scott was one of those whose dislikes were stronger than his likes, he was at his most passionate on things he detested, especially bad wine. Wine was his area of expertise; Terry had chosen from the wine list without consulting him and an absurd argument over degrees of dryness had followed; the smallest of disagreements, as always, provoking the most heated clash.

The second dispute was more serious. Terry had a kind of Daffy Duck voice that he often slipped into, especially late at night, or when drunk: a voice that let things slip that were too embarrassing or too serious to speak of in normal conversation; a voice that could say things from behind a duck-mask, with a fool's frankness. The voice had quacked out its lust for Jenny — his wife's friend, his friend's wife — once too often, the truth half hidden under cover of banter, but this time not sufficiently. The silence that followed revealed something about themselves to each of the four.

That silence seemed to last for minutes. Finally one of two things had to happen: someone had to say, yes, let's do it, let's *swap*, or someone had to say, I think that's enough, you've spoilt the evening. It could have gone either way; Mary chose the latter, reining her husband in.

After the paying of that particular bill, there had been no dinner for several months. And yet even lust for another's spouse was forgivable, and finally easily forgivable; forgiveness was another virtue all four could easily afford.

And the subject was now dead. Despite the odd thigh grope beneath the table, things had developed no further; all four were contented in their marriages; contented enough, at least, to prefer the ease and familiarity of friendship to the disturbances and unpredictability of lust.

It was the third Scene that proved irreparable.

Scott and Terry had always been competitors to some extent. Their friendship had grown through the two women, old school-friends; when the men first met, at university, there had been a long period of verbal jousting, a friendly rivalry that had now settled into a weekly round of highly competitive golf. The dinners usually organised themselves after a Saturday round; or after the 'girls' bridge night', which Mary and Jenny attended within a larger circle of their old school-friends on alternate Thursday nights.

Terry had been an athlete, solid and muscular at school; the good life had filled that athleticism out, it was now a little overfed, reddish-skinned, lumpen. His shirt collars were too tight on his plump neck; the skin of his face had thickened and coarsened. He was known in the hospitals as an athletic surgeon: good hands, quick reflexes, capable of record-time joint replacements — a Hero, in the parlance. Neither intellectual nor diagnostician, he enjoyed most the hands-on stuff, the actual sawing, drilling, cutting. He revelled in massive road trauma: multiple injuries, rapid decision making, all-night operating marathons, actual *physical* challenges.

He always ate red meat. Off-call, beyond bleeper range, he always drank heavily. He often spoke with his mouth full, it seemed to help his Daffy Duck voice. And once — in a crowded Greek taverna — he breathed in as he spoke.

This also seemed to be a performance at first: a duck-spluttery cry for help.

'Gone down the wrong way?' Mary asked, good-humouredly, as her husband began to cough.

Jenny reached over to pat his back, but he had already run out of air to cough with, the cough was swallowed by a strangled sound and suddenly he was on his feet, rearing up, something large and red-faced breaching above the surface of seated diners. His gagging was framed in a total, sudden silence; then people at nearby tables began shouting.

'He's choking!'

'Christ! Somebody help him.'

'Ring an ambulance!'

His face was purpling; he seemed to be trying to say something — perhaps how to help him — but no sound emerged, there was no breath to fill out the words. He took a single step back, then fell forward onto the table in a clatter of glass and cutlery, ripping frantically at his collar and tie.

'Is there a doctor here?' a waiter screamed above the shouting diners, but the only doctor seemed to be choking to death, among broken glass and spilled wine, on a table-top.

It took Scott — usually so quick in court, so decisive, at least with his tongue — some time to react. Or to realise what was happening. Somehow he knew what to do: seizing his bigger friend from behind, balling both his fists in the solar plexus, jerking up and back with all his strength. Something seemed to give, a loosened plug; Terry rolled away onto his side on the wrecked table, a stream of vomit was coughed out onto the floor. For a moment everything seemed to stop again

— waiting, frozen-frame — then he began wheezing, making great sucking sounds, still panic-stricken. Scott forced a finger into his friend's mouth, searching for any further blockage, and was rewarded with a bite; he jerked back his finger with a shout of pain, bleeding heavily.

The ambulance arrived, a stretcher was wheeled in, but Terry was rapidly recovering. He recognised the ambulance officers — foot-soldiers from an army that he usually commanded — and abruptly refused to go with them, sitting off to one side of the table, dropping his head between his knees, still wheezing.

'That might need a couple of stitches,' an ambulance officer murmured to Scott. He flipped open a first-aid box and wrapped the bleeding, bitten finger in an oily gauze.

'I'll be fine,' Scott said, some part of him not wanting to steal the scene from his friend.

He sat down again at the table with Terry and the two women. Around them the restaurant was returning to normal. Their tablecloth was deftly whipped away with all food, cutlery, plates and vomit wrapped inside it; a fresh cloth was flung casually across the wiped wooden surface and drinks and place-settings materialised.

No one seemed able to speak, and at length Terry rose, peeled off a couple of large coloured notes from his wallet, and walked out of the restaurant.

Mary sat for another thirty seconds or so, then rose also:

'Perhaps, I'd better leave too.'

'Of course,' Jenny murmured.

And so they parted, four people who had never, until that moment, asked a single question of the world; had never had reason to. They were innocents, insulated from the kinds of pain that had goaded lesser minds than theirs into better lives than theirs; there had been no real mysteries.

Terry failed to appear at the golf club the following Saturday morning; Scott made up a foursome with some old school friends after waiting an hour at the clubhouse bar. In the afternoon he left a brief, cheerful message on his friend's answering machine, but some sixth sense told him not to press further; especially when on Saturday morning a fortnight later, as he was chipping onto the eighteenth green, he saw Terry on a distant fairway with a couple of total strangers.

Jenny reported home after a bridge night that Mary had merely mentioned that Terry was 'busy', avoiding any further discussion. Mary herself rang Scott after a month, her voice steady as she explained that Terry 'didn't feel up to facing you right now'.

'But I would like to thank you for what you did,' she said. 'Who knows — it might have been serious.'

Scott took some umbrage at this, as did Jenny when he replayed the conversation to her. Her years as a teenage ugly duckling had given her a sharp sense of injustice.

'It might have been *serious*?' she said, in a voice as near to a shout as she ever came. 'You saved his life! Don't they *know* that?'

She planned to make that very point to Mary at the next bridge night, but Mary didn't show; someone's husband was required to stand in at short notice to make up the numbers. The same husband was required again the following fortnight, and the fortnight after that a new member was found to join the circle, permanently.

There were no more restaurant Tables For Four; Jenny's birthday brought a card from Mary, and a brief note — *snowed under with work, hope to catch up with you soon* — which both Scott and Jenny were now able to recognise meant exactly the opposite.

In the small, closed universe of their city all paths intersected sooner or later. Once, Scott thought he saw Terry cross to the other side of the mall, and vanish into a shop as he approached. But there could be no crossing the street when the two men came face to face in a corridor a few months later.

'Terry, how are you?'

'Never been better.'

Scott had halted, but Terry was still moving, almost past him. Scott wanted to reach out to restrain his friend, but hesitated too long. As Terry walked away he made one last attempt to break the ice, turn the taboo subject into a joke, defuse it with humour. Once it was out in the open, he sensed, the problem would vanish.

'Last time I saw you you didn't look so good,' he said.

Terry stopped, and turned. His faced seemed genuinely puzzled: 'Must have been a long time back, Scott.'

And he walked on, leaving Scott standing, flatfooted; but after a dozen paces he turned yet again, and this time shouted, his face purple with anger, as purple as it had been on the night of the Scene:

'What do you want — a fucking medal?'

The words came in a shower of duck-spittle; then he turned on his heel and walked quickly away, and the two men would never speak again.

The Nice
SURPRISE

1

The bus trip to the city was long: eight hours, far too long for only a single 'rest' stop. The queue at the conveniences was also far too long. Beryl Webber — stiff and hobbling, her veins swollen, her throat sore — was the last off the bus and by the time she reached a vacant cubicle the place was a disgrace: urine on the floor, and worse.

She spread lengths of tissue paper on the wet seat and eased her bulk gently down.

Outside, the bus driver began tooting. She sat for a few moments more, panicking, unable to relax, then rose and hobbled outside, her bladder still full.

The stink of that filthy cubicle stayed with her, as if stuck in her nostrils, for the rest of the trip. Her nose began running like a tap, as if trying to wash the stink out, flush it through; her throat felt as if it were burning. She coughed from time to time; her overfull bladder gave a little with each small convulsion.

Raelene was waiting at the bus depot in the city, smiling, helping her down; Beryl determined to do her best by her daughter-in-law this time.

'Merry Christmas, Mother.'

'Merry Christmas, dear.'

A ritual peck was exchanged. The girl *was* pretty, Beryl conceded. Not beautiful, but pretty: her features, small and sharp, might have been pinched out of smooth clay.

The small, pinched mouth smiled: 'You look tired, Mother.'

Beryl coughed again: 'I seem to have picked something up.'

'The bus trip is *aw*ful; you really should have flown.'

'I couldn't afford to fly, dear.'

Raelene glanced at her sharply; she smiled back, trying to hide any accusation. No help with an air-fare had been offered, but then Beryl had expected none.

'Is this all your luggage?'

'And the blue. Over there.'

It was three years almost to the day — Christmas, three years before — since Barry had brought his new bride home from the city to meet her. A week's tense stay had ended unpleasantly in kitchen disputes: accusations, counter-accusations, finally even a deliberately smashed plate. Barry hadn't even *written* for months afterwards, then slowly the letters had resumed — news of the pregnancy, then of the birth.

She hadn't ever seen the child — Darren, her grandson, now two — but loved him from his photographs. He was waiting in the locked car, in the heat. The driver's window was wound open a narrow inch.

'Is it wise to leave him like this, dear?'

'Mother, it's only been a couple of minutes.'

And the child *did* seem fine: fiddling with the gear-shift, clutching a baby's bottle of orange juice. Beryl realised that she had broken her resolution already. She tried to backtrack, to control the damage.

'He's so much like you, dear,' she lied.

In fact she could see only Barry, her own son, in those clear eyes and small, fine, elf-ears.

'I'd better not kiss him,' she said, 'he might pick something up.'

She eased herself into the passenger seat with some

difficulty, then fumbled in her handbag and turned and tempted the child with a chocolate bar she had brought for exactly that purpose. He wedged himself in the furthest reach of the back seat, watching suspiciously.

Raelene climbed into the driver's side. 'No chocolate,' she said. 'Please, Mother. He's allergic.'

The car backed out of the parking bay and turned onto the road. Once again Beryl couldn't help herself: 'Shouldn't Darren be wearing a seat-belt?'

This time the impatience in her daughter-in-law's voice was unmistakable: 'It's only a couple of blocks.'

Driving without a seat-belt seemed far more dangerous to health than eating chocolate, but Beryl managed to hold her tongue. She twisted her neck as far as she could towards the child, and smiled crookedly: 'Do you know who I am?'

The child sucked at his bottle of juice, watching her.

'Is that the Witch?' he asked his mother.

Beryl's eyes filled instantly with tears; she turned her face to the window and fussed with her handbag, hiding the chocolate bar back among the tissues and pads and hairpins, hiding the tears from her daughter-in-law. But finally she was forced to say something; the hurt had been spoken too clearly, too loudly, to be ignored.

'Is that how you speak of me?'

'It's nothing, Mother. We all say things we don't mean.'

Barry was home from work when they arrived. He came out to meet the car, hugging her briefly with what could have been embarrassed affection, or merely ritual politeness.

'How are you, Mum? Tired?'

Despite everything, despite the trip, her bladder, the

chocolate, the hurtful words in the car, the sight of him still filled her with a sudden pang of love. He was still — he would always be — the small, snow-capped boy who ran out of school towards her each afternoon, his schoolbag flapping around his neck.

She found a smile for him, easily: 'Nothing that a cuppa wouldn't fix.'

'How was the trip?'

'A bit long,' she said, and restrained herself, trying to avoid any tone of complaint. 'Nice through the mountains. In places.'

Raelene and the child had vanished inside; Barry jerked her luggage from the boot and she followed him into the house.

'You look thin,' she said. 'Are you eating?'

He forced a laugh: 'Don't start, Mum.'

It was ridiculous — exactly the kind of thing she had planned not to say. Yet he *was* looking a little peaked. There were other worrying signs: the house itself. A Dream Home, certainly — at least when built. Nothing much seemed to have happened since. The sofa was second hand, and wearing thin. Rugs covered the cement floors, not carpets. And her guest room, the child's room, had makeshift curtains: bedsheets, of all things, thumb-tacked to the window frame ...

She bit her lip as Raelene made up the bottom bunk, saying nothing.

'There, Mother. I hope you'll be comfortable.'

'I'm sure I will, dear.'

'It's a bit cramped. We had nowhere else to put you.'

She locked herself in the clean, scented sanctuary of the toilet for a time, a long time, then rejoined the family in the kitchen where Raelene was pouring out the tea.

'You've got the house looking very nice, dear.'

'I don't really have the time,' Raelene said. 'What with working. Milk, Mother?'

'Working?'

Raelene poured out the milk: 'Three days a week. At the salon. Sugar?'

Beryl took her tea black, with three sugars, but other things seemed more important to discuss: 'You take Darren with you?'

Barry was on hand: 'Don't worry, Mum. There's a woman down the road. She looks after several of the local kids.'

Beryl could sense their eyes meeting across the room, somewhere beyond or behind her. And perhaps it was *that* — that sense of being patronised — that irked her. Suddenly she couldn't help herself. All resolve, all diplomacy, vanished.

'Are you sure that's a good idea? The boy is still so young. Shouldn't his mother ...'

Raelene was instantly up and on her feet, banging cupboards, clattering cutlery from here to there, and back to here.

'Mum,' Barry said at length, 'if this is going to work, we're all going to have to try a *lot* harder.'

Silence.

'I think I'll get an early night,' she said, and coughed, and felt her bladder, not yet fully emptied, give again. 'I caught something in the bus. All those bodies crowded together.'

2

Christmas morning everything seemed changed, transformed into a higher, more perfect state. There was a feeling of truce in the air, a willingness to overlook the past: troops emerging from the trenches to share gifts. Was it the day itself, the occasion, the spirit of the season? Or was it the video camera that was attached to Barry's shoulder from first light? Certainly each time the machine began whirring, smiles widened, the volume of laughter increased, the family members seemed warmer to each other, their behaviour more ... choreographed.

'Merry Christmas, Mum,' Raelene said, pressing a kiss onto her cheek as she joined them around the tree, the more formal Mother for once dispensed with.

'Smile, everyone,' Barry muttered for the hundredth time from behind his whirring, compact machine.

'Mewwy Chwistmas, Gwanma.'

Darren's lisp, usually barely perceptible, also seemed exaggerated for the camera — a cute child-star's lisp — but at least he was smiling. The three adults watched indulgently as he fought his way through the thick-ply layers of wrapping paper, unearthing a succession of electric trains, brightly coloured clothes, huge soft toys. There may have been no curtains in the house, but there was a video camera and a mountain of gifts. Beryl felt pleased at her own modest choices. Her gift to the child — a book — was among the first he examined, and discarded. She felt confident he would come back to it. For Raelene she had brought an oven-mitt in the shape of a giant lobster claw; for Barry the usual socks.

'Sensible socks,' he said, good-humouredly, and even Beryl laughed at the phrase.

In return she received a set of soaps of different fragrances, in some sort of expensive paper wrapping.

'Very nice, dear,' she murmured to her daughter-in-law.

'Barry chose them,' Raelene smiled back. 'I ran out of time.'

This exalted state lasted into lunch, the video camera still whirring from time to time, into its second, or third, cassette. Even the sorry excuse for Christmas dinner — chicken instead of turkey, salads, no ham, a tinned pudding to follow, a *bought* pudding — failed to dent Beryl's tolerance. A single glass of bubbly went to her head; she left the table soon after the pudding and lay down on her bunk-bed for a time.

When she emerged late in the afternoon the video camera had been zipped away inside its black bag; the child had broken several toys and was in a tantrum; the atmosphere had darkened and thickened. Barry was trying to repair a section of electric toy-train-track; Raelene was in the kitchen, plunging and clattering dishes noisily in the sink.

'He seems overtired, dear,' Beryl called above the noise. 'Shall I put him down?'

'Stay out of it, please, Mother.'

Beryl remembered the chocolate bar in her handbag; she ferreted it out and offered it to the child: 'I'm sure a bit of chocolate won't hurt once. It's Christmas, after all.'

Raelene emerged from the kitchen and snatched the bar: 'Christ! You just can't *help* yourself, can you? You have to interfere!'

She stomped from the room, slamming the door after her. Barry continued fiddling with the screwdriver for a few seconds, then flung it down and stomped off himself.

'Christmas fucking day!' he shouted back. 'Why does it always have to end like this?'

Only the child remained, suddenly silent, out-tantrumed by his parents. Beryl found some ice-cream in the fridge and a box of stale, crumbling cones on a shelf; soon the boy was licking sleepily, tranquillised like a lizard by the coldness.

She thought: time for a lie-down. The word described it exactly; there was seldom any sleep. The child was soon asleep in the top bunk, but Beryl tossed restlessly below. Her face seemed to be burning; the pillow soon grew too hot; she turned it over, enjoying, for a time, the temporary coolness. The dark side of the moon, her late husband had liked to call it.

She must have slept; she opened her eyes in darkness. Heated voices carried from the next room, the master bedroom, which must have woken her. She strained to listen, hearing, or imagining, a few loud, discernible words — 'chocolate', 'the Witch'. Slowly the raised voices softened, first a low muttering, then a murmuring, then finally — past midnight, the red glare of her clock-radio told her — came the sound of bedsprings, rhythmically bouncing. She heard Raelene cry out with pleasure, and suspected her daughter-in-law of making extra noise for *her* benefit.

Then there was silence.

She fiddled with the clock-radio till she found some city equivalent of the music she listened to at home: Music for Easy Listening. The child was breathing easily, softly, above her, but she couldn't join him. The tiredness of the trip had been slept off, she was stranded in her usual night wakefulness, the insomnia of age that all her widowed friends shared, an insomnia that sometimes seemed an unwillingness to sleep, a reluctance, or refusal, to enter even a temporary unconsciousness.

And whenever she might have drifted off, her cough jarred her awake: infrequent, but just frequent enough.

3

'Slept well, Mother?'

The makeshift curtain had been tucked aside; Raelene's voice reached her through a dazzle of light.

'I don't think I slept at all,' she said.

Raelene was dressing the child, spinning him this way and that as she slipped various clothes over him. He was pliant in her grip, rubber-limbed, still half asleep.

'It's a wonder I didn't keep you all awake with my coughing.'

Raelene wasn't interested in complaints; she was already half out of the door: 'Didn't hear a thing.'

Barry poked his head through the door a few minutes later before he left for work.

'Feeling better, Mum?'

'I think I've a bit of a fever.'

'Probably just the heat,' he said, and stood shifting from foot to foot at the door, not so much giving reassurance as seeking it.

'Perhaps I should see a doctor,' she said.

He laughed: 'You'd never get in, Mum. This is the city. You have to plan your illnesses months ahead if you want to see a doctor.'

She managed to smile; he grinned back: 'We'll make an appointment later in the week. If you don't pick up.'

That settled, he moved on to a more important subject: 'Um ... I forgot to ask you last night, Mum — but I knew you'd agree. It seems silly paying the girl down the road while you're here. Could you keep an eye on Darren today? We're both off to work.'

Her breathing suddenly felt tighter, more constricted, hemmed in: 'I don't know if I'm up to it, dear.'

'You'll be fine. Plonk him in front of the TV. Rae should be home around three.'

He was gone before she could protest further. Raelene failed to reappear; two car doors slammed in the drive, not quite in unison; an engine gunned into life.

She rose with difficulty, and, after checking the child, bathed with even greater difficulty, although for a time the steam seemed to clear her congested chest. Soon, though, the tightness returned, and she began shivering uncontrollably. Of course the child refused to cooperate; ice-cream failed to tranquillise him this time but she came across the confiscated chocolate bar pushed to the back of a shelf and handed it down with a trembling hand.

'I've a nice surprise,' she smiled, weakly, as he snatched.

He showed no sign of gratitude, or even affection; happiness was no more than the absence of a tantrum, or the losing of himself in daytime television. But then Barry had been much the same; she felt a rush of love for the child anyway, or at least for those elf-eared parts of him that so closely resembled his father.

She was back in bed, shivering beneath the sheets, when Raelene arrived home at five. The house was a mess of toys, spilled drinks and smeared food, but at least the child was asleep, exhausted by a day's hard havoc.

Raelene brought in a cup of tea and a couple of aspirins and was almost sympathetic until she found the empty chocolate wrapper clutched in Darren's sleeping hand. Her small, sharp features pinched even tighter.

'No wonder he was so hard to control,' she shouted. 'Chocolate sends him crazy! For God's sake, don't you *ever* listen?'

4

Barry drove her to the hospital at midnight, overruling his wife's insistence that it was nothing serious, nothing that a couple more aspirin and a good night's sleep wouldn't fix.

'Nerves,' Raelene diagnosed. 'She's worked herself into a state.'

The doctor at the hospital — young, and brusque in manner — disagreed.

'Pneumonia,' he pronounced, somewhere at the edges of Beryl's fog of delirium. 'How long has she been like this?'

She was trembling uncontrollably, and breathing with difficulty, but this last accusation — directed at Barry — she heard clearly. She *was* sick.

The doctor's face was the first she saw as the fog cleared. Her breathing had eased, a whole day has passed — or so she was told. The ward was windowless; the lighting artificial, there was no way of orienting herself.

'When can I go home?'

'Not yet,' he told her. 'When the X-rays clear a bit.'

He held a stiff, plastic transparency in front of her, pointing out various dark shadows and fluffy clouds as though he were proving something.

'You'll be very weak for some time, Mrs Webber.'

Barry visited each evening, sitting and chatting uncomfortably at her bedside; but Raelene and the child failed to appear.

'I should be home soon,' Beryl murmured from time to time. 'Doctor says it won't be long now.'

Her son talked awkwardly past the subject each time she raised it, switching to other matters: hospital food, his job, the past. On the subject of home he always failed to meet her eye; his visit would develop a hurried and nervous feel to it.

On the fourth day she felt the need to pin him down: 'I *can* come home, can't I?'

His eyes moved past her, he was addressing a spot just above her head: 'Mum, I've spoken to the doctor. There's a convalescent home. Greenglades. You could stay there till you're ready to travel. We both feel you might be better off.' His words hurried on: 'Also, I've bought an air-ticket. I don't want you going back in the bus.'

'Well, if Doctor says ...'

'The doctor agrees the home would be good for you.'

She paused, thinking: 'Is it far from you?'

His eyes came back to hers, relieved: 'A bit further than the hospital. But I can visit every day.'

'And Darren? I've hardly seen the boy.'

His eyes shifted back to the wall: 'He's been very upset, Mum. What with everything. And this place ...'

'Then I'll ring,' she said, and added proudly: 'I'm walking to the end of the ward now. Tomorrow the lobby. There's a payphone.'

He seemed alarmed: 'Um ... You mustn't ring, Mum.'

A coldness filled her suddenly; a strange, tingling dread. Once again he was addressing the wall above her head.

'I don't know how to say this, Mum.'

She waited, holding her breath.

'I was hoping I wouldn't have to tell you.'

His eyes strayed even further up the wall, wandering erratically. Finally he took a large breath, and spoke: 'Darren thinks you ... passed away.'

Was that all? Her dread vanished; she watched him, merely puzzled.

'Was I *that* sick?' she said. 'You must have been very worried.'

'We were Mum. *Very* worried.'

She sat a little higher in the bed, smoothing the sheets: 'Well, won't it be a nice surprise for the boy when you tell him.'

He began speaking rapidly again, phrase following phrase, heel and toe: 'How can we do that, Mum? Rae told him you'd died ... It was stupid, I know. She regrets it now. She was in a rage. The chocolates. Everything else ...'

Beryl tried to picture the scene: the child worrying about his grandmother, badgering his mother into that final explosive lie.

'You *were* nearly dead,' Barry ploughed on, defensively. 'Lucky to make it through the night, the doctor told us.'

She finally got a word in: 'I'll ring up and put him straight.'

He was aghast: 'Mum, what would he *think*? That you'd come back from the grave?'

She puzzled at this for a moment before speaking again: 'Then it's up to Raelene to put it right.'

'Mum, we think it's best this way. For the time being. Leave things be. At least till he's a bit older. It's a difficult age. We don't want the child confused.'

His eyes slid away again, into some corner of guilt, or perhaps merely shame.

'You mean I can't see my own grandson?'

'Perhaps not till he's older, Mum.'

But I might be dead by then, she almost added. *Really* dead. She turned away herself, gazing beyond him, her eyes unfocused.

'Well, I'd better be off,' he stammered. 'The office ... I'll look in tomorrow.'

He made an attempt to smile; realised it was pointless, even pathetic, and rose and walked away. She watched him to the end of the ward, trying to remember that small boy with his flapping schoolbag but seeing only an adult, an ordinary adult, shambling and plump.

'I might ring him up,' she called after him, suddenly, defiantly.

He didn't turn, perhaps didn't hear, and she raised her voice even further, threatening: 'I might ring any time! As a surprise!'

But even as she shouted she knew the threat was empty; knew that the boy was safe, that he would hear no voice from beyond the grave.

Pointing
THE BONE

1

The phone rang on the brink of midnight, jerking Nick back from the brink of sleep. He fumbled, automatically, for the receiver, somewhere on the bedside table in the near-dark. His mouth also moved automatically: 'Nick Harvey.'

'Nick — I hope I haven't woken you.'

Nick knew the voice, or knew that he knew it, but for the moment seemed unable to locate the name.

'I'm sorry,' he mumbled, still drugged with sleep. 'Who is this?'

'Nick, it's Philip. Philip Tandy. I know it's late, but it's important. I'm trying to track down a horrible rumour.'

The words splashed his ears like cold water; he was instantly awake. He sat up in bed, but carefully, leaving the reading lamp off, trying not to wake Cassie, his wife.

'It's about Anthea,' the voice continued. 'A horrible lie. I wondered if you'd heard it?'

Nick was cautious, noncommittal: 'I heard something. It was all a bit vague.'

'I thought you might have. I've just been speaking to Josie and David — they seemed to think they first heard the rumour from *you*.'

Nick was dumbfounded: 'When was this?'

'A few minutes ago,' Philip said. 'I've just got off the phone to David.'

'No, when was I supposed to have told *them*?'

'At some school function. A month ago. They are certain it came from you.'

Nick shivered in his warm bed, momentarily lost for words.

This was simply not true. In fact, the *opposite* was true: he was certain he had first heard the story from Josie. But what could he say? His closest friends had already turned him in; it seemed petty, given the gravity of the rumour itself, to quibble. And he *had* passed the rumour on — not to his friends, perhaps, but certainly to his wife. And through her to other friends. He *was* guilty, if not precisely as charged.

'I'm sorry to put you on the spot, Nick — I need to know who told *you*.'

'I'm not sure, it was a few weeks back.'

He was stalling, wondering what he could say that would get him off the hook. Who could he finger to escape prosecution himself?

Philip was insistent: 'It's important, Nick. Very important. Anthea and I want you to understand that there is no truth in the story at all. None whatsoever. We're both surprised you would choose to pass it on without checking with us first.'

This accusation was true — he hadn't thought to check. But how *could* you check? How could you even mention it to Philip and Anthea?

'It's a terrible and cruel thing to do to Anthea. We have no idea how it started. Or from whom ...'

Philip paused momentarily: Nick was given to understand that he was among those being considered for the position of Whom.

'Naturally we want to stamp the story out as quickly as possible. Before any more damage is done.'

Nick found his tongue again: 'Breast cancer, was it?'

He almost asked: *is* it? At the other end of the line Philip fell silent again, unwilling, perhaps, to acknowledge the bluntness of the word. Cancer. Or perhaps refusing to allow the substance of the rumour any kind of airing, refusing to legitimise the details, even by rebuttal.

Cassie stirred in the darkness next to him, he sensed her turn and stretch: a small gust of warm woman-smell, released by the bedsheets, carried to him. A heavy sleeper, she always took some waking. Those two whispered words — Breast Cancer — had penetrated more effectively than any early morning alarm.

The voice on the phone continued: 'As you can imagine, Anthea is *very* upset.'

Nick could imagine, all-too-easily: Anthea Tandy was a legendary hypochondriac among her circle of friends. Was it always the case: the fate of those who cried wolf?

He shivered again, guiltily: where were these cruel thoughts coming from? It wasn't her fault that she had contracted cancer. Except that she hadn't contracted cancer after all. Possibly.

'I would appreciate it,' Philip was saying, but more with tired anger than appreciation, 'if you could contact anyone you might have told, and tell them the truth.'

Beside him in the half-darkness Cassie waited, now wholly awake, listening to one half of a conversation, waiting to hear the other as soon as he hung up. Beyond her the clock radio glowed, sole light source in the dark room, four red digits: 12.04.

'Okay, Philip,' he said. 'Yes, I'll do that. Look, I'm sorry for any distress. I really am.'

As he spoke the words, he realised that he didn't quite believe Philip, that his sorrow was still for the victim of cancer, rather than for the victim of rumour. He tried to force himself to believe.

'Give my apologies to Anthea. I hope she can forgive us all. Let's get together soon ...'

2

Nick had first heard the story from Josie Wells when picking up the children from school.

The school mothers gathered at the school gates from 2.30 each afternoon, a good half-hour before the school bell released their little darlings. The School Gate was something of a social occasion, and also a catwalk: the women dressing up, competing a little with each other. Not in opera best, perhaps, some even still in tennis whites or brights, fresh from suburban lawn courts, but always well groomed. And crisp. One of only a handful of fathers at the school gate — running a mail-order business from home, liberated from office hours — Nick was permitted honorary membership in the group. He was not required to compete, or even step onto the catwalk. Nor was he required to speak much, but he liked to listen. Mostly the gossip had to do with the performances and private lives of the various teachers, with petitions to sack this or that piece of dead wood, with negotiations on who could stand in for whom on the tuckshop roster.

He remembered the afternoon of the cancer rumour clearly. Silence had fallen as he approached the group; it took some time for the story to emerge. Breast cancer — a woman's cancer — seemed too intimate a subject to share with a man.

But of course they had all wanted him to know, eventually:

had allowed him to guess his way through various evasions and half answers without too much difficulty.

'Of course you *must* keep it to yourself, Nick,' Josie urged.

The first person he told was Cassie, when she arrived home from the clinic that night. She immediately spent an hour on the phone, ringing around various friends: 'checking', she claimed, defensively, but it seemed to Philip that she was doing more talking than checking.

As far as he could remember this had been his sole crime: telling his wife.

'You awake?' he asked as he guided the phone by feel back into its cradle.

'Of course I'm awake. Tell me.'

'That was Philip. He says that Anthea has *not* got cancer. The rumour was a lie.'

She switched on the bedside lamp, dazzling him, and sat up, propped on her pillows.

'What do you mean? What did he say — exactly?'

'Just that. What I said. Anthea has not got cancer.'

'No, I want to hear *what* he said. His exact words. Start at the beginning ...'

But the phone was ringing again. Cassie tried to reach past him but he was too quick.

'Hullo?'

'Nick, you're awake? It's Josie. I'm sorry about the hour but it's important. Something's come up.'

'Let me guess — Anthea Tandy.'

'Shit! His Philip rung you already?'

'Just off the phone.'

'I'm sorry. Really. We dumped you in it a bit.'

'Nice friends. I heard the rumour from *you*.'

'No Nick, it was at the school quiz night. You told us.'

'Josie, it was at the school gate.'

Cassie wrenched the receiver from his grasp before he could finish, and began to talk.

'Can you *believe* he would ring ... Really? He rang them too? ... He must be ringing everyone ... like a chain letter. I wonder where he'll end up ... not here, thank God ... of course, I don't blame him. Imagine how Anthea is feeling! No, I couldn't face her ... If it's *not* true it's almost as bad.'

Nick took up this last odd nuance with her when she had finally finished, some minutes later.

'What do you mean: "almost as bad"?' he said. 'If she hasn't got cancer, what does it matter?'

She seemed surprised that he didn't understand: 'How would *you* feel if people believed you had cancer? Wouldn't it make you ... uneasy?'

'It wouldn't worry me in the slightest. I haven't got cancer.'

She reached behind her and touched the varnished wood of the bedstead, disturbed: 'Don't tempt fate, Nick.'

He had seen this in her before, often; it never failed to fascinate. Her years of nursing training suddenly jettisoned, she was back in the world of witchcraft. Usually it was confined to the kitchen: a magical belief in the powers of certain vegetables, juices, yeasts. Full-blown voodoo was rare.

In fact she was the most rational of her clan. Witchcraft seemed to have been handed down the female side of Cassie's family like a cottage craft: family get-togethers rarely finished without a discussion of dream messages, star signs, the healing properties of crystals. Cassie at least had retained a sense of humour about such things. Once, when he had caught her tossing salt over her shoulder to assuage the fates after some misdemeanour, she had laughed and said that of *course* she didn't believe in magic.

'Then why do it?'

'The good thing about magic,' she had said, teasing him, 'is that it works even if you don't believe in it.'

3

Nick argued against a visit to the Tandys — the 'mercy dash' that Cassie suggested, too jokily, the next weekend. They should 'let things settle down', he told her.

'Josie says Anthea's losing weight,' Cassie reported a few days later.

'Cassie!' he warned.

'Maybe it's the worry.'

'I don't think we should talk about it,' he said, firmly.

She laughed: 'And you call *me* superstitious.'

'It's nothing to do with superstition. It has to do with good manners. Especially after the phone call. Philip's word is good enough for me. She isn't ... ill. I don't even want to speculate about it.'

He managed, successfully, to force the matter from his mind. The Tandys weren't present at the next Third-Sunday-of-the-Month tennis afternoon; he refused to join in the discussion that this provoked among those who were present, Josie Wells chief among them.

A week later Nick heard that the Tandys had left for a

holiday in North Queensland: just the two of them, Philip and Anthea, *sans* children.

'Strange time to take a holiday,' Cassie mused, 'in the middle of the monsoon season. Josie says they spent their honeymoon there.'

Nick was having none of it: 'Should be wonderful,' he said. 'Away from all this innuendo.'

The Tandys returned from Cairns a month later; a fortnight after that Anthea died. None of the friends had visited during those two weeks; no one had heard from her; no one even knew she was ill. Nick and Cassie first heard the news when Josie rang on a Monday morning, having stumbled across the death notice in the morning paper.

'So soon?' Cassie hissed into the phone, shocked, as Nick watched from across the breakfast bar.

Cassie flipped her own paper over to the back section, and scanned the obituaries. Nick listened, breakfast forgotten, as the two women compared versions by phone, line by line, as if trying to find some sort of inconsistency, or typographical error, that might disprove the terrible fact:

'Died suddenly at home after a short illness. Dearly loved wife of Philip, mother of Josh and Amber ... A short illness? And why wouldn't he admit she was dying? Josie, we've been their friends for *years.'*

Nick and Cassie inserted their own tribute in the paper the next day; it appeared in a column of similar tasteful tributes beneath a larger, black-bordered funeral notice. There was much phone and school gate discussion among the circle of friends during the next two days over whether to attend. What would Philip expect? What would Anthea have wanted?

'Of *course* we're going,' Cassie eventually decided, repeating the words, several times, if differently inflected, to various callers on the phone: 'Of course *we're* going.'

At the chapel all seemed forgiven. After the ceremony Philip hugged both Nick and Cassie in turn, thanked them warmly for coming — and murmured a hope that they would 'come back to the house afterwards'.

It was a small gathering: a scattering of family members outnumbered by a dozen or so friends, Josie and David Wells among them. Philip moved among the small people-clumps with trays of sandwiches and glasses of wine: occupying himself, deliberately it seemed to Nick, with the logistics of hospitality.

He seemed 'remarkably composed' to Josie. David Wells expressed the opinion that Philip had clearly been 'mentally preparing himself' for months. There was a smugness in the tone of this that irked Nick, he soon excused himself 'needing a refill' and attached himself to another smaller group.

After some time he realised, slightly startled, that only the friends remained. Anthea's only sister had left, taking Philip and Anthea's two young children with her. Laughter could be heard from some of the groups; the mood of the gathering seemed more relaxed. Josie, even less able to hold wine than gossip, dropped her glass, as usual, which smashed. David, perhaps to distract attention from her, slipped a CD into the sound system: 'Best of The Supremes', an ancient favourite of Anthea's.

As Josie, on hands and knees, gathered the glass fragments, people began to move their heads and tap their feet in time to the soul music.

'This is the way Anthea would have wanted it,' David shouted across the room. 'This is how she should be remembered.'

This seemed more than a little impertinent, in Philip's house, but the mood of the gathering had lightened, and various Anthea-anecdotes began to be exchanged, more or less in humorous vein. The bereaved husband might not have been smiling, but there was no trace of disapproval as he uncorked two bottles of champagne, and filled a close-packed array of slender glass flutes on a tray. He exchanged, methodically, a foaming flute for the empty or half-empty wine glass which was clutched in each hand, then switched off the music, and stepped onto a small footstool, raising himself above the gathering.

The hubbub of voices dampened and ceased, his friends formed a circle about him, smiling, supportive, curious — and eager to play their part in whatever ceremony, or tribute, he planned.

'I'd like to congratulate you,' he said.

One or two puzzled glances could be seen among the smiles.

'You killed her,' he stated, simply. 'All of you.'

Someone reached out a restraining hand, and whispered to him.

He shook himself free: 'No — I won't calm down. I can't forgive you. You *willed* her into the grave — all of you. You willed her to have cancer. You ... *voted* for it. It was like — like she was elected, or something. An election by gossip. Well, this is your election night party. Congratulations — you won.'

Around the room the friends were looking at each other,

aghast. And yet not quite looking at each other: as soon as their eyes met, glancing away in embarrassment. David Wells, never one for holding back, came to their rescue:

'Fair go, Philip. I know it's been terrible for you, but try and be fair. She had cancer before anyone began to *talk* about it.'

'Maybe. But as soon as you all stopped believing that she would live ...'

With this, his composure vanished; his voice faltered, his body shook. He stepped down from the footstool into someone's arms: Cassie's.

'I'm sorry,' he was muttering to her as Nick approached. 'I'm sorry.'

She murmured something indistinct; Philip raised a tear-smudged face: 'It's ridiculous, I know. But I can't seem to stop thinking it. The more you try not to think it, the more you think it.'

'It will pass,' she said. 'You might not believe it, but it will.'

'I don't *want* it to pass.'

She enfolded him in her arms, holding him tightly for a moment, a fleshy mattress in which he could muffle his sobs, then as he recovered she led him from the room, searching for somewhere private.

Nick followed, listening to his wife's comforting platitudes, not knowing how to help. He stood awkwardly in a bedroom doorway as Cassie helped Philip onto the bed, and sat next to him, holding his hand, brushing the tears from his face with her fingertips.

'I remember lying in bed at night as a child,' Philip was telling her, 'lying there trying desperately not to think certain things. Certain ... words, or phrases, that forced themselves into my mind: *I hate God. I hate God.*'

'We all used to do that, Philip.'

'But I was obsessed. I would whistle to myself, recite stories and multiplication tables — and still the words appeared.'

A half smile squeezed for the first time through his tears: 'For a few weeks, at the age of eight, while this obsession lasted, I was sure I was going straight to hell.'

Nick, listening, was returned to his own boyhood, to his first flight in a jet plane: a trip he would never forget. A stewardess had seated him at a window as a treat, but as the plane detached itself from the earth he had screwed his eyes tightly shut, unable or unwilling to believe that the enormous metal object, this much-heavier-than-air machine, could defy the law of gravity. His older sister, seated next to him, taunted him, telling him that if he didn't believe, then the plane *wouldn't* stay up. The combined willpower of all the passengers was the only force that kept the plane aloft, she teased.

He spent the entire flight with his eyes closed, teeth tightly clenched, concentrating, trying to believe — and whenever he began not to believe, whenever a small doubt began to find voice in his mind, he would sing, or make loud noises, and block his ears.

As Cassie comforted Philip, touching his cheeks, bathing him in whispers, Nick stepped backwards into the hall, averting his face, overcome by guilt.

Tea and
MACAROONS

1

Miss Doris Simmons had taught at School — the word would always be upper-case in her mind — for almost fifty years. Age-ceilings had been overlooked: she was an institution, a physical fixture, as much a part of the School grounds — the actual scenery — as the Olive Pearce Memorial Hall or the Jennifer Pendry Gates.

She had not raised the matter of retirement herself, or even owned up, publicly, to a single birthday, for a decade — suspecting that the School board, and Joan Retallick, the Headmistress, preferred to neglect the fact that she was nearing eighty. She had no intention of reminding anyone. Her health was good, her small frame so slight and dainty that there was simply no flesh, she sometimes felt, for illness to work *with*. Her mind was active, and things had never been better for the School science staff.

Which consisted, mostly, of Miss Simmons.

She sat at her desk in the empty chemistry laboratory — throne-room of her small empire — gazing out across the surrounding hockey fields. Late afternoon sunlight drenched the world; the grass seemed as smooth and green as billiard felt. She felt content, even serene: a recent gush of federal funds to private schools had allowed the building of the new laboratory, and although only one senior girl planned to pursue the subject into her final year, Doris eagerly anticipated the challenge. The girl, Heather Metcalf, was the Open Scholarship winner and the first in fifty years to take a science subject that far.

Science would never be big at School, of course. Art, music, literature, history — and hockey and horse agistment — were higher priorities for most of the girls, many of them boarders from the country.

They had chosen a Ladies College, after all: priding itself — preening itself — as something of a finishing school.

Miss Simmons glanced at her watch, then out again across the sunlit hockey fields towards the Memorial Hall: almost simultaneously all three members of her leaving chemistry class — Heather Metcalf among them — emerged from the arched doors. She savoured this part of the year especially: the weary sweetness of another journey's end, the last hurdle crossed, the girls arriving at her desk with their public examination question papers, excited, flushed, eager to check the correctness of their answers, which were already en route to the central board of examiners.

As the girls crossed the playing field they were already comparing papers. Miss Simmons watched as they huddled momentarily, heads together, haloed from behind by the afternoon sunshine. Their voices carried, in snatches, across the even, rolled grass, and through the open window of the laboratory: *Me too ... What about this one? ... I thought it was a trick question ...*

At length, Heather Metcalf detached herself from the group and walked away towards the school gates, shaking her head. Miss Simmons watched her favourite leave, puzzled, and a little disappointed. The other two girls entered the laboratory, chattering, slapped a question paper on the desk before her, and bent about her, one at each shoulder.

'An oxide is a calx, isn't it, Miss?' Prue, the taller girl, asked.

'Why don't *we* call them oxides?' the other, Susan, asked simultaneously.

'It's how I was taught, dear. Heather isn't with you?'

'Her mother was waiting,' Prue said.

Susan giggled. 'The dreaded Frau Metcalf. Did you see that *hat*?'

Miss Simmons never encouraged this sort of talk: 'Was Heather happy with the exam?'

'It's hard to tell with Heather,' Prue said. 'What about Question Eight? What's atomic number?'

Miss Simmons slid her reading glasses from their small compact case and slipped them on.

'I'm surprised to find it here,' she murmured, after reading through the question several times. 'It sounds like the kind of question that belongs in a Physics paper.'

'That's what *I* said,' Prue announced. 'Didn't I just say that, Suzy?'

Miss Simmons attempted to steer the conversation back to the student who most concerned her. 'Did Heather mention anything? Any ... problems?'

'She said she had never *heard* of some of these questions,' Prue said.

'You can't expect to know *all* the answers,' Susan added, dismissively. 'She's never satisfied.'

Miss Simmons refused to be drawn into any alliance against the absent girl. 'It doesn't matter how hard an exam is,' she murmured. 'It's the same for everyone.'

Reassurance was not required. She knew that, to both of them, finally, their studies were in part a game: they had taken science, or happened into science, almost accidentally. Neither was pursuing chemistry into her final Matriculation year. The girls wanted to know the correct exam answers — they wanted to know the *score* — but merely as a way of ending this particular game. Their excitement was transitory: the excitement of the hockey field, of the equestrian water-jump.

'Everyone is in the same boat,' she added, unnecessarily, speaking more to the absent student, she realised, than to those present.

2

She used the same words to Heather Metcalf on the phone that night, unable to wait until the morning lesson to hear how her best student had fared.

'Everyone is in the same boat, my dear.'

Her favourite was not so easily placated. 'A friend at my old school,' she said, 'Sarah Anderson, she knew all those answers. She *laughed* at me when I said I'd never heard of atomic number.'

'But that's physics, dear, not chemistry. I don't think it's fair to put such questions in a chemistry paper.'

The girl failed to reply, and after a short silence Miss Simmons found herself talking too much, trying to fill that silence with soothing noises, excuses, and even apologies. When she finally managed to stop herself talking, the silence was still there.

'We'll do better next year,' she tried again. 'I'll study the Matriculation syllabus over Christmas.'

'You mean you don't *know* it?'

'You're my first,' she said. 'I'm looking forward to it. It's a great challenge for us both. Don't you agree?'

Her enthusiasm failed to be transmitted by telephone: the girl did not sound convinced: 'Well, I *suppose* ...'

'As for the exam, don't put too much store on first impressions,' Miss Simmons counselled. 'I'm sure you did much better than you think. *Much* better. Besides, it's next year that counts. I think we can achieve something very special together.'

She eased the conversation into unrelated areas — Christmas gifts, holiday plans — but after hanging up sat for some time at her small phone-table, feeling uneasy and a little empty. The girl had been more talkative towards the end, but there was something missing from her tone: a lack of warmth. Was it a mistake to ring again? Perhaps, but she couldn't help herself. She reached for the phone and dialled, wanting to reassure herself more than the girl, wanting to go to bed untroubled.

A man's voice answered, and told her, politely enough, that his daughter was in the shower and couldn't come to the phone. Miss Simmons suggested that she might ring back later; there was a slight pause in which he seemed to be talking to someone else, or taking instructions, then he told her, still politely, even pleasantly, that Heather was 'a little overwrought', and both he and his wife felt that 'it might be best if she was left alone tonight'.

Disturbed, Miss Simmons retrieved from her case the copy of the exam paper that Prue had left with her, and spread it on her escritoire. She brewed a pot of tea, slipped on her reading glasses, sharpened an HB pencil, set out a clean note pad and began to write out answers to the questions, realising, quite suddenly, halfway through the exam, that she herself, the teacher, would only have achieved an average result, that certain areas of the syllabus had somehow evaded her attention.

3

She was summoned from the laboratory to Miss Retallick's parlour the following day. Her three students were in the throes of producing carbon dioxide from a Kipps' apparatus, and bubbling the gas through lime-water. The experiment was straightforward, even elementary: end-of-year fun and games. She left Heather Metcalf in charge, hoping the responsibility would lift her sullen mood.

The girl's parents were seated in the parlour; she recognised them, vaguely, from a previous parent interview night. That is, she could not have put a name to them if she had met them in the street, but in context she remembered having met them before: she was *reminded* of them. Her memory was fine, everything was safely filed, somewhere — it just needed prompting at times. The father appeared as mild mannered as he had sounded on the phone the night before; the mother — compact, smiling without warmth — was clearly more formidable. Miss Simmons sensed that she was the driving force, the engine room of this marriage.

Both parents rose and shook her hand, the mother staring directly into her, the father unwilling to meet her eye: she felt another twinge of unease.

Miss Retallick was smiling: 'A small problem seems to have arisen, Miss Simmons. Mr and Mrs Metcalf are concerned about the recent examinations.'

'I think it's a bit early to pass judgement ...'

The Head overrode her, politely firm: 'They have even raised the possibility of withdrawing Heather from School. Of course I have assured them that such a drastic step would be unnecessary, that we could clarify and rectify whatever problems have arisen.'

A knock at the door preceded the entrance of the school secretary with a tray of tea things: silver service, the Royal Doulton crockery, and a plate of macaroons, an institution that had survived various changes of headmistress.

Miss Simmons remembered her own first interview in the parlour, at the age of twenty-five, fresh from teachers' college, applying for the position of Science Mistress. Headmistresses had come and gone since — had come and gone several times — but the customs remained. Rumour had it that appointments to School staff were still made on how well an applicant handled her cup of tea and macaroon at that first crucial interview.

The macaroon was the more important test: the ability to nibble daintily, dislodging no crumbs.

The mother refused the offered plate, but the father seized a macaroon. Perhaps he was nervous: he ate like a scholarship parent, clumsily, without evidence of breeding. His wife, as if in sympathy, spilled a little of her tea into the saucer: it seemed strange to Miss Simmons that she would never have been offered a position in the School, yet the School was begging her to allow her clever daughter to remain.

'We brought her here because we thought she would do better,' the mother said. 'She wants to study medicine ...'

'She's always wanted to be a doctor,' the father intervened, smiling weakly.

Miss Simmons felt it was time to speak up again: 'I think we should wait until the results come out. The paper was very difficult — it is the same for everyone.'

She chose a macaroon, and nibbled as Miss Retallick took over her defence: 'Miss Simmons has been in charge of science teaching at School for many years — there have never to my knowledge been any previous complaints. I think we should rely on her judgement. We all feel that Heather has settled in remarkably well at School, academically *and* socially. She is such a wonderful *asset.*'

The father seemed mollified almost immediately, the mother required another cup of tea, poured by the Head, and several further flattering sentences. Finally Miss Retallick sensed that there had been some sort of change in the mood.

'Perhaps we should allow Miss Simmons to get back to her class. I'm sure you both agree that the best course is not to rush into any precipitate action. At least until the publication of results.'

The Head smiled towards her; as the smile hardened, Miss Simmons realised, too slowly, that it was a smile of dismissal.

She rose and shook the hands of both parents, but looked at the mother as she spoke: 'She will do very well next year. I plan to study the Matriculation syllabus myself over Christmas ...'

She realised, immediately, that once again she had said too much. The door closed behind her, she stood for a moment outside, wanting to re-open that door and try again, this time choosing her words more carefully. But it was too late; she brushed a small flake of macaroon from her breast and walked away, knowing that further discussions would take place behind closed doors, behind her back.

4

She granted Prue and Susan an early minute; surprised, they walked away whispering, glancing back.

Heather wouldn't meet her eye. She stood on the other side of the workbench, fussing with the apparatus: bespectacled, slightly built, intense. Gas bubbled through a milky solution between them, ignored. Outside, the other girls moved across the green hockey fields towards the main building: two high bird voices, two golden, glowing heads. A lump clogged Miss Simmons's throat: the view through that open window suddenly seemed more like a painting of some heightened, idealised childhood than a view of anything real: soft-focus, impressionistic, something remembered rather than seen.

Something that was already lost.

The warm late-afternoon air, hazy with fine grass particles and dust, began to tickle at her nose. She sneezed, and the force of the small explosion sent her tottering backwards. She shut the window — shut out the summer, and the departing voices — and turned to the girl.

'If you leave, I'll have to leave too,' she said, simply.

'I'm sorry,' the girl said, after a pause, still averting her eyes.

Anger flared in Miss Simmons for the first time: 'I must say I had hoped for a little more loyalty.'

A thought occurred to her: perhaps the girl was not suitable for School after all, not up to the demands and sensitivities that were required.

'An education involves more important qualities than academic excellence,' she added.

Tears filled the girl's eyes, magnified by her thick pebble-lenses: 'Miss Simmons, what else can I *do*? I want to study medicine. I need good results. I'm not going to get *in* if I stay here.'

And Miss Simmons realised, clearly, for the first time, that she was asking too much, far too much; she was horrified at the words she had spoken.

'I'm sorry,' she said. 'Of course you're right.'

The girl looked directly at her teacher, blinking through her tears, surprised.

'Maybe I *could* stay,' she said, 'if we worked together. And here, in the new laboratory ...'

'No,' Miss Simmons said firmly. 'You should go. *We* should go.'

The girl rose and came to her, and they hugged, and stayed locked together for a moment, the girl's face resting on her shoulder.

'I'll never forget you, Miss Simmons,' she said, a phrase the teacher had heard from her favourite charges at the beginning of summer each year for the last fifty years, but now, she realised quite suddenly, for the last time, as the bell rang outside, and the chemistry lesson was over, and all the years before it.

Tuxedo
JUNCTION

1

'You've ruined it! *Ruined* it!'

The customer wasn't a regular. Nor did Graham recognise the jacket dumped angrily on the counter: a glistening tux. Not many tuxedos came his way. It was the kind of suburb that hired formal suits, he had realised soon after he bought the dry-cleaning franchise. Now, a year later — a year too late — he could draw a line through the city: a frontier between those suburbs that owned dinner-suits and those that hired. He had chosen the wrong side.

The shouting continued: 'You thought I wouldn't *notice*? You thought you could get *away* with it?'

He was a big man, gone fleshy: an ex-footballer perhaps, paunchy, short necked, standing shoulders back and legs apart, carrying his excess fat with cocky pride, as if it were still muscle. A semi-retired school bully, Graham guessed, remembering the type all too well.

'I'm sorry,' he murmured. 'But I'm not sure what you're talking about.'

'*This* is what I'm talking about.'

The big man thrust the jacket in his face. A burn mark gleamed on the tail flap, the unmistakable imprint of an iron fused into the dark fabric.

'I really don't recall seeing this suit before.'

The big man shook his head, contemptuously: 'You guys!' A small moustache twitched on his coarse, puffy face. 'So predictable. I ought to *deck* you.'

'Do you have your docket, Mr ...?'

'Fuck the docket. My wife brought the suit in last week.'

Graham examined the clothes the big man was wearing: a baggy Puma tracksuit, Saturday morning pull-ons, one small step more formal than pyjamas. He had never seen the man before, but he often recognised various clothes walking about the neighbourhood. He tried to match a woman's face, a wife's face, to the tracksuit.

'Does your wife have the docket?'

His tone was polite, unruffled; something told him to take it easy. He knew he wasn't the culprit — he hadn't pressed a tux in a month. It wasn't hand-iron country anyway, but steam-press. He decided to play along a little, to follow normal procedures. Everything by the book.

'She's misplaced it,' the big man said. 'Surely you keep a record?'

'Of course. When did she collect the suit?'

'Friday. For a wedding. I had to wear it like *this*.'

Graham reached below the counter for the previous week's receipt books.

'Name?'

'Frogmore.'

Now he placed the wife. She came in almost **daily**, hidden behind some great wodge of trousers or sports **coats**, silk shirts or tennis shorts: all the various male uniforms, business and leisure. There something shy and mousy about her — always peeping from behind, or beneath, those clothes. Graham had difficulty picturing her face. She rarely brought her own clothes: the occasional difficult stain on a blouse, and a recurring pants suit, the only such outfit she possessed, it seemed.

He remembered mainly this: that she couldn't stop talking

about her husband as she separated his laundry tenderly, lovingly, on the counter. No other subject escaped her lips.

'He needs these tomorrow,' she would say. 'And these for the weekend. He's flying to Sydney. His work often takes him interstate.'

There was something beaten down about the woman, Graham sensed, something doggy, faithful ... and peripheral. But what a mountain, an *alp,* of business she brought in.

As he faced her angry husband Graham remembered that weekly alp — and how badly he needed it. His first year had been a struggle: rent hikes, lease payments on the new Per-Cleaner. It occurred to him to fake a confession: to hand over the price of a new jacket without argument. To argue the point and lose that business would surely cost him more.

'I can't seem to find the docket,' he stalled.

The big man reached across the counter, spun the receipt book, and began flicking through.

'Very convenient,' he sneered. 'Two sets of books, or what?'

Graham's tone was placating: 'If it's my fault, I'm only too happy to replace the suit. But repairs might be possible. Leave it with me. And if your wife could bring in the docket, it would help.'

'I'll be in touch,' the big man said, or threatened.

2

His wife walked through the door the next morning, a pair of tartan trousers draped over her arm. She seemed unwilling to meet Graham's eye.

'His golfing trousers,' she murmured, eyes fixed down. 'He loves his game of golf.'

'Where does he play?'

'Henley. He is club vice-captain this year.'

His. He. Him. There was something reverential in the way she spoke the words, like a pronoun heard in church.

'When would you like these?' Graham said, scribbling the docket.

'Thursday?' she mumbled, already heading for the door.

'Ah ... One other thing, Mrs Frogmore. Before you go.'

She half turned, but still her gaze refused to intersect with his.

'Yes?'

'Your husband mentioned you might bring the docket. For the tuxedo.'

'The tuxedo? Yes, of course. I'm sorry. I've searched everywhere. I can't seem to put my hands ...'

She paused, and shrugged weakly, and then was through the door, walking fast. Graham pinned the duplicate to the golfing trousers, and routinely searched the pockets. His fingers slipped through a gaping hole in the right hand pocket. He snorted, recalling a cheat he had known some years before at his own less salubrious golf club: a retired police inspector, another big man, who always carried a spare ball in his pocket for slipping down the trouser leg at crucial moments. He twiddled his fingers in the hole in those golfing trousers, remembering, wondering.

No, *hoping*.

3

She was back on Thursday for the golfing trousers. Even when she wasn't carrying a load of laundry she somehow seemed hidden, avoiding his gaze, standing side-on.

'I found a hole in the pocket,' he murmured as he passed across the pressed tartan pants, hung in a sheath of clear clinging plastic. 'I sent them for repairs. Free of charge.'

She stood, shifting from foot to foot.

'And the tuxedo?' she finally asked. 'Have you been able to repair that?'

He stood behind the counter, saying nothing, until her eyes finally met his.

'No luck, I'm afraid. Are you sure you brought it here?'

'What do you mean?'

He lifted the hinged section of counter and beckoned her inside: 'Let me show you something.'

She followed hesitantly. The tuxedo was hung near the ironing board, behind the tumble-driers. He slipped the coat from its hanger, draped it across the narrow board and pressed a cold iron over the burnt, fused patch. The burn-mark and the iron clearly didn't match.

'Square peg in a round hole,' he said, and added, unnecessarily: 'It wasn't my iron that did the damage.'

She turned away from him abruptly, covering her face in her hands. Her shoulders heaved, although she made no noise. He found a box of tissues somewhere and offered them, awkwardly, offhandedly:

'You burnt the coat yourself?' he prompted.

She nodded, jerking a succession of tissues from the box,

balling them and dabbing at her eyes.

'I didn't mean to blame *you*,' her words came with difficulty, between sniffs. 'It was the first thing that came into my head. I hate arguments — and he gets so angry sometimes.'

Graham stood clutching the tissue box, wondering whether he should touch her, wrap a comforting arm across her shoulder, or whether such acts might be misconstrued.

'I didn't think he'd come *in*,' she said. 'I planned to replace the suit myself.'

'And tell him it was from me?'

She shrugged, and dabbed at her eyes again.

'Sit down,' he said. 'I'll make some coffee. You can't leave here looking like that.'

She sat obediently, as if used to taking orders: a small pinched woman in a dowdy cotton shift, clutching her husband's tuxedo jacket.

Graham busied himself in the partitioned kitchen area: filling the electric kettle, sniffing the milk, swirling a little hot water in the bottom of the empty coffee jar to release the last stuck grains.

He was glad to be free of her, temporarily. She was still within earshot, yes, but the flimsy hardboard partition offered an excuse for silence.

'He said to tell you,' she called, loudly, through her sniffles, 'he'll be in on Friday for his money.'

Or His wrath shall Descend, Graham whispered to himself.

'Milk?' he shouted.

'Please. No sugar.'

'Sweet enough already?' the glib, irrelevant phrase seemed to speak itself as he emerged from behind the partition.

'You're not having one?' she asked.

'Had too many already today,' he lied.

She sipped, then attempted — with some difficulty — to smile, to lighten the mood: 'Do you run a counselling service for all your customers?'

'Only the good-looking ones.'

He was flirting with her now, no doubt about it. And yet not intentionally. He just didn't know what else to say: these standard male responses seemed the only pleasantries, the only words of cheer he could find.

'Look,' he said, before anything else slipped out, 'I'd better get some work done. But stay as long as you like.'

She set down the mug, half empty, and rose: 'No. I must be going.'

Her usual worried, harried look — momentarily cleaned from her face as she sipped the coffee — returned.

'What are you going to tell him?' she asked. 'He wants the money in person. And a proper apology.'

Graham laughed. 'Wants a ceremony, does he? A humble-pie ceremony? Perhaps we could videotape it.'

After a short silence, she laughed with him — uncertainly, perhaps, but one of the few times she had allowed herself a laugh at her husband's expense, Graham guessed.

'You give *me* the money,' he suggested, 'and I'll hand it to him. With a thousand sincere apologies. Anything to keep the peace.'

She reached into her handbag for a chequebook and pen, scribbled out the figures, using the ironing board as a base, and detached the cheque. She hesitated, then stretched on tiptoe to kiss him lightly on the lips:

'You're a lovely man.'

And then she was quickly gone, embarrassed. As he fingered the cheque Graham doubted he would see her again, or her weekly heap of business, no matter how lovely she had thought him. Briefly, he considered spilling the beans to her husband, if only to receive an apology from *him*. But no, she needed all the help, all the protection, she could get. And the more he thought about it, the more he was beginning to look forward to the ceremony. He would be acting a lie, perhaps, but there was pleasure even in that: a shared, illicit pleasure, a kind of cheating, or verbal cuckolding, a conspiracy with a wife that would gratify him more than any sexual cheating could have, as he looked that big, important bully in the eye, and lied straightfaced to him, and paid him off with his own worthless money.

The Booster
SHOT

1

Years had passed — more years than Alison cared to count — but she recognised him immediately.

Her thoughts were elsewhere, he was the last thing on her mind, but the red flame of his hair singled him out across the crowded airport lobby, raised his face as if in haute-relief from a background frieze of faces.

He hadn't spotted *her*. He was pushing through the crowd, approximately in her direction, glancing back across his shoulder. A woman she had never seen before was at his side.

'Blue!' Alison called across the lobby. 'Blue! Is that you?'

The man turned as she approached, and smiled, and opened his mouth to speak — but the woman at his side spoke first.

'You obviously haven't seen Philip for some years,' she said.

'I'm sorry?' Alison stopped in her tracks.

'No one calls him Blue any more.'

'I don't think you've met my wife,' Blue intervened. 'Suzi — Alison Tully. You must have heard me talk of Alison?'

The wife offered her hand, limply. It was thin: a smooth, fashionable claw, encrusted with various configurations of cold metal and precious stone.

'I don't think so,' she murmured, and smiled, although the smile was also something of a murmur.

Blue was not quite so thin; still red haired — source of the nickname that had fallen out of favour — and pale-skinned, and with those clear, childlike eyes. But there was a new puffiness to his face and cheeks. Alison recalled a boyish tennis-player, a Finn or a Swede, pale and puffy-faced, she had watched recently on television who, at the time, had reminded her of Blue.

'And this,' Blue turned, 'is little Sebastian.'

For the first time Alison noticed the small child tacking a loaded luggage trolley awkwardly back and forth across the lobby behind his parents. Of course Blue would have children by now, but she was still shocked; and to some extent shocked that she was shocked. Part of her was obviously not yet ready to grant him permission to father children with anyone else.

Even after all these years.

She bent and examined the child: 'And how old are *you*, Sebastian?'

The child's lips remained pressed together, a tight purse.

'Sebastian is five,' Blue answered for him. 'Aren't you, Sebastian?'

Alison forced a smile. She wasn't comfortable with children; she found the conversations that took place in these circumstances inane. She tried to summon back some other noise from the standard adult-to-child repertoire.

'Have you come to Adelaide to visit your grandma?' she came out with.

'We've come to see both our grandmothers, haven't we?' Suzi informed her.

Alison felt her hackles rise, slightly. She suddenly remembered another Suzi she had known, years before: a school enemy who when she signed her name had always dotted her i's with a cute little circle. It was unfair, of course, but already she had lumped the two Suzis together.

'What are you doing here?' Blue asked.

'Seeing Brian off. To Sydney for a conference.'

'Brian?'

She paused, sensing that he too was a little shocked by the dislocation of an ancient world picture. He also remembered her as he had last seen her: frozen in that time, that place. There were still things in the air between them, she realised; a faint perfume of accusation, and guilt. There had been no clean break, after all; more a slow rending, a long, jagged tear.

'Brian is my hubby,' she said, using the ridiculous word for some reason she couldn't identify.

Blue smiled: 'Of course.'

'How long are you here for?' she asked. 'You must have a meal with us. Brian would love to meet you.'

Aware that she was addressing only Blue, she half turned to include his wife: 'Both of you.'

The woman spoke again: 'We're only staying the long weekend.'

'Then you'll miss Brian,' Alison said. 'But come anyway. You must come. Tomorrow night. Or the next, whichever suits.'

'Give us a call,' Blue said. 'We'd love to come. Wouldn't we, Suzi?'

Suzi was preoccupied with removing the luggage trolley from the tight grasp of little Sebastian.

'Where are you staying?' Alison remembered to ask as they moved away from her into the crowd.

Blue turned: 'At Mum's. Still remember the number?'

If she did, she wasn't prepared to admit it publicly.

'It's in the book,' she said. 'I'll find it.'

2

The table, a big, carved mahogany bench, a family heirloom, had always been too large for Alison's tiny dining room. The three of them sat clustered at one end, like the last descendants of a once-great family. Suzi had brought flowers: a clutch of daffodils that spilled upwards and outwards from a vase on the far end of the table.

Sebastian was asleep on Alison's bed; the wine and reminiscences were flowing freely. Even Suzi, so remote and suspicious in the airport lobby, had loosened up. Alison had deliberately worn no make-up, and dressed herself in what Brian liked to disparage as 'gardening' clothes: a shapeless jumpsuit. The tactic had worked. Suzi has obviously decided there was no threat from *this* former girlfriend, still childless, but already gone to frump.

'Everyone said that Alison and I were meant for each other,' Blue was telling his disbelieving wife, 'when we first met at university.'

She laughed: 'I couldn't imagine two people more different.'

She was beautiful in a dollyish sort of way, Alison conceded: big eyes, small, upturned nose, hair teased thickly as if to render the head proportionately larger and more childlike.

'No, really,' Blue was telling her. 'It was incredible. We might have been twins.'

'Separated Siamese twins, we liked to tell people,' Alison said, and laughed herself, glowing inside with a warmth that was only partly due to the wine.

She remembered the game they had often played when they

first moved in together, guessing how close they must have come to meeting each other in their childhoods, trying to fix actual dates and places when they must have passed within inches of each other, unknowingly.

'I played Joseph in my kindergarten nativity,' Blue, increasingly garrulous, was telling his wife. 'Alison played Mary in hers, same day, same year, a single suburb away. She was head prefect of her girls' school, me of my high ...'

They had sat in the same audiences for interschool debates, in the same crowds at combined sporting events, and had never met. But fate had no need to resort to accidents, to chance collisions in the street. Their separate paths were always going to cross at university.

'Those were golden times,' he said, and seemed about to add something, but checked himself. *The best times of my life*? The words seemed implicit in his hesitation, or was it just wishful thinking on Alison's part: these were the words she wanted to hear? She poured out another wine, drowning, half tipsy, in nostalgia. She suddenly wished she had dressed up a bit, or performed a more careful cosmetic miracle — tried to remind him of what he had lost.

'So what went wrong?' Suzi said, half tipsy herself, impervious to any undercurrents.

Suddenly Alison had no idea what had gone wrong, or why it had ended. She felt Blue's foot gently pressing against hers beneath the table, and knew he was wondering the same thing.

'What went wrong, Blue?' she held his pale gaze a moment too long.

He increased the pressure of his leg: 'Nothing that I remember. I guess we should still be together.'

Suzi chortled, secure in her girl-charms: 'Don't let me stand in your way.'

'I'll get some coffee,' Alison rose from the table.

'I'll help you,' Blue offered immediately.

He picked up a couple of plates and followed her through the swing door into the kitchen, and immediately set down his plates and seized her from behind and pushed himself hard against her back.

'When can I see you?' he whispered, pressing his lips to her ear.

She half turned her head, rubbing her cheek against him: 'I'll be home all day tomorrow.'

Then he released her, and they carried out the coffee things and she was forced to sit with the width of the absurdly big mahogany table between them for the rest of the evening, allowed only the teasing pressure of that leg.

After he had left she groaned aloud with desire and impatience, her threshold of pleasure as low, she felt, as it had ever been: a hair-trigger. It was midnight, and she was drunk, but she rang Brian in his hotel room in Sydney, waking him and inveigling him into a conversation of obscene suggestions and longings: the thrill of long-distance vicarious sex tinged only slightly with guilt that she was using her husband for the first time ever as a surrogate.

3

'I've a bone to pick with you, Blue,' she said.

He watched her with his clear, Finnish eyes, surprised.

'Remember that book I gave you? On your nineteenth birthday?'

They were sitting each side of the big table again, just the two of them. The spontaneity of the night before was gone; he had kept his distance since arriving, having second thoughts perhaps. Had he made love to his doll that morning, she wondered? Worked his lust out of his system? She felt vaguely irritated — and remembered for the first time how irritated he had often made her in the past. His mood swings, his unpredictability.

She offered another clue: 'A book of poetry.'

Still there was no response. The sun poured through a northern window, unobstructed, weightless. Vapour from their two coffees eddied lightly and mingled where it entered the light.

'It had an inscription in it,' she added.

'I *think* I remember,' he answered cautiously, slowing his speech as if sensing some kind of conversational radar trap ahead.

'I found it after you left for Sydney,' she said. 'I was in a second-hand bookshop. And there it was.'

He groped for an excuse: 'They printed more than one.'

'Not with your name in it. In *my* handwriting.'

He screwed his eyes shut, and grimaced: 'Oh, shit.'

'I was *very* hurt, Blue.'

He made an attempt to explain: 'I had to leave town in a hurry. There was no time to pack. The company found me a place in Sydney, but it was too small. And they only paid part-relocation costs. I had to sell everything. Jesus. Ali — I didn't think.'

'I had to order that book from America, specially.'

She decided not to tell him the rest of the story. How she

had gone home from the bookshop and angrily dug through her treasure drawer, removing everything of his. His photos and love-letters. The soap she had kept for years since their first love-making: the perfumed soap they had used, together, lovesick teenagers, in the motel bath afterwards.

He tried to regain some sort of initiative: 'I've a bone to pick with *you*,' he said. 'You never wrote to me.'

'*That's* why I never wrote to you,' she told him. 'Because of the book. I couldn't believe you would do such a thing.'

And instantly she felt safe from him — or from herself, from the drunken lust that had overwhelmed her the night before. The fire was dead, and could not be rekindled, not in the sober light of day. Other memories were coming back to her: the real memories, she suspected. A kind of morning-after immunisation was taking place.

She knew he felt the same, but suspected also that he would still go through the motions of desire, halfheartedly, out of habit. Or to save face. Especially now that she seemed reticent. He could never resist a challenge.

'What about last night?' he asked, and pressed her foot again beneath the table.

She removed her foot: 'What about it?'

'You felt something.'

'I felt drunk. It wasn't real.'

He seemed a little stung by this: 'Hubby is real?'

She was stung herself by the way he flung the strange word back at her, and even more by the fact that he had stored it up all night.

'Just as real as Suzi,' she answered, and then couldn't stop herself. 'Tell me — when she signs her name, does she dot the i with a cute little circle?'

She couldn't believe her luck when he hid his face in his coffee cup, saying nothing.

'She does!'

After some time he looked up to face her, and smiled: 'I'm sure Brian is a wonderful man. You seem very content. I wish I could have met him. And told him how lucky he is.'

He had always had this knack, she remembered, of finding the right thing to say: of spoiling her anger, turning it back on herself, ruined, altered, loaded with guilt.

'I'm sorry,' she apologised. 'I shouldn't have said that. About Suzi.'

'You haven't seen the real Suzi,' he went on. 'I guess she felt a bit threatened. I've talked so much about you since the airport.'

She tried to hide her pleasure in hearing this: 'Another coffee?'

He shook his head and rose from the table: 'I must be off.'

'Before you go,' she said, 'I've something for you.'

She rose herself, and reached behind her and took a slim book from a drawer in the sideboard.

'Here — I'll give it to you a second time.'

He opened the book to the flyleaf and read the inscription.

'I'm sorry I sold it,' he said. 'I can't tell you how much. That was wrong.'

Apologising also had never been a problem for him. If he was wrong, he accepted it easily. She had loved this at first: she had never seen it in other men. But later ... well, he was so *often* wrong.

'I'll be checking all the second-hand bookshops,' she smiled, trying to make light of her mixed feelings.

They walked to the door arm in arm, and she opened it, and he stepped out and glanced up and down the street.

'How are you travelling?' she asked.

'I borrowed Mum's car.'

'Where is it?'

'Around the corner.'

His eyes slid away from hers, sheepishly, before he added: 'You can't be too careful.'

Hearing this, her heart, still a little wayward from the night before, finally aligned itself with her head: she could almost hear a click. None of his smooth flatteries or apologies could change the fact that it was over. There could be no second innocence, no forgetting, no unlearning.

Or none at least without alcohol.

She suddenly wished she had been more friendly to Suzi, less jealous, more sympathetic. She might even have warned her of the sweet-and-sour road ahead, warned her that life with a man who was well practised in parking his car around corners, out of sight, might not be all it seemed.

But then surely Suzi already knew.

He bent and tried awkwardly to kiss her on the mouth. 'Bye, Ali.'

'Goodbye, Philip,' she said, and offered only her cheek.

Jesus
Wants Me For
A SUNBEAM

'In us we trust.'
JOHN BERRYMAN

1

Richard and Linda. Benjamin and Emma. To outsiders, the Pollards seemed more a single indivisible organism than four separate members of a family: a symmetrical unit.

Examined from any angle, that unit presented the same number of faces to the world: mirror faces, crystal faces. Two adults, two children. Two females, two males. A father, a mother. A son, a daughter.

Simple statistics, perhaps — unimportant, even trivial, in themselves — but to Rick and Linda they were an emblem of something larger: of the balance, the harmony, the self-sufficiency of their lives. It seemed to the young parents that not much else was needed, that *any*thing else — a third child, for instance — was somehow excessive, disproportionate.

Ungeometric.

'One of each,' friends remarked, enviously, after the birth of their second. 'You're so *lucky.*'

Linda feigned chagrin at this: 'Credit where credit's due, please — it took years of careful planning.'

She was not entirely joking. If their good fortune was not exactly planned, it was, she felt, at least deserved. It was earned.

More symmetries emerged as the years passed, equally unplanned — or, at most, half planned. Often these were merely whimsical: that both adults were Capricorns, both children

Sagittarians. Other symmetries seemed more significant, or meaningful; or even useful: that father and daughter were left-handers, mother and son orthodox, would surely make for exciting doubles tennis in future years.

The more such facts came to light the more both parents actively sought them out. It became a family game, from which data that didn't fit were excluded, or conveniently ignored: that both children had been dealt their father's mud-brown eyes, for instance.

Their mother's were blue: a pale, sky-blue.

Rick and Linda had been happy themselves as children, sheltered in the leafier avenues of the city. They came from solid families, grew up in nice suburbs, attended good schools. Solid, nice, good: these were the specifications of their world, largely interchangeable, universally applicable. They met at a suburban public library, as teenagers, studying for final school exams, and felt their way cautiously into love. They discovered sex, equally cautiously, through each other, and only through each other: a slow, almost courtly process of escalating excitements spread over many months.

They married while still at university. It seemed a precipitate step, the first missed beat in a measured rhythm — both sets of parents were agreed on this — but the young couple, pimple-spotted, barely extricated from their teens, smiled their way past any objections. Strengthened by each other, they had grown immune to parental advice, they could, they found, outlast it. Both now knew that they were halves of something bigger, that their lives before — their 'previous lives', Rick joked — had been incomplete.

They married in St Paul's, Linda's parish church. They chose the recently arrived Reverend Cummings as celebrant — a young student-priest, or priest-intern, whom Linda had met through the church youth group — rather than the older rector that her parents preferred. Bill Cummings was their own age; he permitted a revised modern set of vows in which both partners promised to love, honour and cherish, but from which the ancient assymetrical duty of wifely obedience had been deleted.

The young couple salvaged a few dusty, spidery pieces of furniture from the cellars and backsheds of their reluctant families, and rented a small student-flat in the inner-city suburbs. To their families it seemed that they were still playing at being grown-ups, that their tiny, cramped flat was not far removed from the doll's houses and backyard cubbies of a few short years before. Both sets of parents offered the support of weekly meals and monthly pocket-money. At times, as if bidding against each other in some auction of allegiance, they even offered help with house-cleaning and laundry.

'You won't have *time* with all your studies, dear,' Rick's mother urged her new daughter-in-law. 'Why don't I pick up a laundry basket each week?'

'Rick does the laundry, Mother,' Linda said, a little smugly. 'You'll have to speak to him.'

The older woman was incredulous: '*Rick* does the laundry? But he's never washed a thing in his life.'

'He's a quick learner.'

To Rick and Linda it was the beginning of a shared adventure. Snuggling to sleep each night after love-making, it seemed terrible to both of them to have been forced to sleep all those years apart, alone, in a narrow child's bed. It seemed like something out of Dickens, Linda's favourite bedtime reading: a cruelty that happened to orphans. Each evening after lectures they took long walks together through their new neighbourhood, holding hands. Each night they shared a steaming, brimming bath. They chose items from the morning paper, which they read to each other over breakfast, as if feeding each other handpicked delicacies. They packed frugal student lunches, which they ate on the library lawns together between lectures. Each Saturday they played mixed doubles in the local Club competition; each Sunday they pedalled their pushbikes — their old school bikes, refurbished — long-distance, visiting families and friends. Their physical resemblance to each other, near-identical height and body-build, seemed to become more pronounced through those first years of marriage, as if eating the same food and sharing the same exercise caused an even closer convergence of body-types. Without exactly planning it, Rick permitted his hair to grow a little longer, Linda cropped hers shorter; they chose, independently, similar gold-rimmed glasses. They often wore each other's T-shirts, and even, at a stretch, before the birth of Ben, each other's jeans.

Their shoes-sizes alone refused to converge, although lying together in bed — naked, limb-entwined — they would occasionally compare bare feet, and pretend, playfully, that there had been some shrinkage or enlargement.

'Is that your foot or mine?'

'Wriggle your toes.'

'It must be mine. But it doesn't *look* like mine. It is my right foot or my left foot?'

'Perhaps you should have them engraved.'

Two years of bliss followed the wedding — the years before the birth of Ben, their first child — but when they looked back on those two years later, their lives, once again, seemed to be lacking something. Even the memories of those early days of awkward, thrilled sexual discovery faded, even the milestone of their graduation from university, and their first appointments as teachers in the same suburban highschool, now also seemed to belong to a previous life: Life Before Ben.

The birth was premature, the labour difficult, the baby undersize. Afterwards Rick sat on the edge of his wife's bed, holding the tiny, scrawny bundle with great care.

'He's very beautiful,' he said, 'for a frog.'

Linda clutched at her sore stomach, groaning with joy: 'Don't make me laugh, *please.*'

The frog refused to sleep. He croaked and sniffled and wheezed. He regurgitated more food than he ate, but still filled an endless succession of nappies at the other end of his sewer, refuting all known laws of the conservation of matter. And, always — and more always at night — he cried. He *screamed.* To Rick and Linda, still surprised to find themselves parents, energised by astonishment and excitement, these trials seemed no more than rites of passage, small sufferings that were more ritualised pleasure than pain: trials half dreaded but also half hoped for, expected, *imagined,* and therefore surmountable. Once again there was no end of outside help through these trials: both pairs of grandparents competed with offers of daily child-minding. Linda's mother, a volunteer worker for Meals-on-Wheels, once even dropped off a spare meal for the young couple at the end of her weekly round among the pensioners and disabled.

'Leftovers from the kitchen,' she explained, defending this small corruption. 'We would only have thrown it out.'

It was thrown out, but only after she had left. The thought counted, Linda declared, even if the food was inedible.

The world that surrounded the young family seemed charmed; every face that turned towards them was smiling, wishing them well, offering help. Their neighbours — Greeks, mostly, in their inner-city suburb — showered them with baby gifts, and honey-cakes, and pastries drenched with icing sugar, and incomprehensible advice. At school their fellow teachers were benignly tolerant of late arrivals and missed classes. Even the occasional hurried escape from a Church sermon with a howling baby on Sundays was warmed by the glow of a hundred tolerant, knowledgeable faces — and a pause and patient smile from the Reverend Cummings high in the pulpit.

His boyish, slightly podgy smile seemed to bestow on them God's personal, unspoken benediction.

2

Their world was charmed and protected, but not ignorant: news from beyond the municipal limits filtered through. That the lives of others might not be so charmed was clear to them, at least in abstract. They dropped generous donations into the Church Christmas Bowl and Easter Appeal each year; they fostered a World Care child in Bangladesh after the birth of Ben, and after Emma's birth fostered another in Ecuador.

Once a year a Christmas card and letter arrived from each child, written with obsessive neatness in Spanish, or the weird extra-terrestrial script of Bengali. Typed, misspelt English translations always accompanied both letters, their tones identically flat and formulaic despite their separate origins, as if written by the same child, or by a computer. Snapshots were sometimes clipped to the letters, and perhaps these were also of the same child: a small bony waif, dressed in ill-fitting Best Clothes, probably an older sibling's, posed in front of a squalid shanty. They decided not to answer these letters. It seemed demeaning, even humiliating, to compel a child to write thank you letters, to report annually to its benefactors — to beg, in essence. It seemed best to keep at some sort of distance. They sought no gratitude themselves. Nor did they seek knowledge. Their quarterly donation was to *prevent* misery, not to learn about it. Payments were debited, automatically, invisibly, against their bank account.

'I can't see the point in torturing ourselves with details,' Linda argued. 'As long as we do our best to help. Don't you agree?'

After the birth of Emma she refused, suddenly, to go to movies for similar reasons — disturbed, she explained, by their increasing violence. This pronouncement, again, caused no argument from her husband — their minds, moving in tandem on most issues, had converged again on this. She had merely put their joint thought into words.

The thought was waiting to be spoken by one of them, its final choice of mouth was unimportant.

To some extent the film-boycott was academic: their two infant children permitted no time for movie-going. Ben reverted to his earlier, more demanding state with the birth of his sister: waking at night, refusing food, vomiting at will whenever his rival received too much attention. House-moving added another upheaval to his life. The family had outgrown a narrow student-house; with help from grand-parents, a loan for the deposit, they took out a mortgage on a small villa a little further from the city and a little closer to the suburbs of their childhood.

Linda's boycott of the television news a few months after moving house was not so academic. The decision was reached, or cemented into words, on a late summer Sunday evening. The young couple had arrived home after a long day of tennis, tucked tired children into early beds — *trapped* them in bed, bound beneath tight sheets — and settled themselves in the television nook with shallow silver trays of Chinese take-away. Was their mood too tranquil, too pleasantly weary, too resistant to any disturbance? The lead story on the news was surely no more horrific or blood-spattered than usual, but Linda shivered — suddenly, involuntarily — and averted her eyes from the screen.

'How horrible,' she said, and turned to her husband. 'Turn if off. Please.'

He hesitated: the evening news was a ritual he enjoyed, a warm shower at the end of the day. Its actual content was somehow less important than the comfort of the form: a cathode-ray squirt of images, a steady horizontal stream that washed through his tired mind. As he wavered, Linda seized the remote control and waved it at the screen; a talking head contracted to a bright pinhead, then vanished, a genie sucked back inside its bottle.

'Why do they *show* things like that?'

For once he felt the stirring of an argument: 'Because it happens, sweetheart.'

'Why can't they show good news for a change? The million *good* things people do every day? They always choose the one bad thing.'

'Perhaps we should try to understand it.'

'How can you *understand* it? A man who murders his entire family, then himself!'

She shuddered again, as disturbed by her own blunt summary of events as she had been by the original story.

'Maybe he did it out of love,' Rick suggested, weirdly.

She stared at him, incredulous: '*What?*'

He watched the blank screen, as if waiting for more information, trying to understand this odd germ of a thought, to *grow* it.

'Misplaced love,' he said, groping. 'If you're depressed, and the world is not worth living in, you want to save your loved ones from it. You want to protect them.'

He paused, caught her astonished eye, and added hastily: 'Maybe.'

They sat in silence: Rick even more stunned than his wife, mystified by the origins of these words that had jumped from his mouth, unpremeditated. He poked a wad of rice into that mouth, and chewed, allowing himself a little thinking time.

Linda saved him from further inspirations; she came up with a more convincing theory: 'I think it's merely selfish. They want someone to go *with* them.'

Rick swallowed his food. 'Like the Egyptian pharaohs,' he said, 'taking their whole households into the pyramids, buried alive.'

Their thoughts were back in harmony.

'Or the rajahs in India,' Linda said, and shuddered again,

remembering a movie she had seen as a child, 'burning their
wives on their own funeral pyres.'

She rose, moved down the hall, and softly, protectively,
closed the doors to the bedrooms where the children slept.

'This is morbid,' she whispered as she returned. 'How did
we get on to this?'

'The news.'

'Let's talk about something else.'

Her husband resisted one last time, momentarily; still
tantalised, perhaps, by his earlier heresy: 'I know it's
unpleasant, but should we turn our backs on the world?'

'If we can't change it, what's the point? I don't want to *know*
about those ugly things. I don't see why I should have to.'

She watched him, waiting for agreement.

'We do what we can,' she reassured him. 'We do our bit.
Why should we thrust our noses in it?'

She was right, he knew. You had to draw chalklines, erect
barricades. There was so much pain and misery in the world
you would drown in it: a great ocean of pain, of which the
cathode-ray tube sprayed only a few selected drops in their
direction. With the zeal of a fresh convert, or a fresh runner in
a relay, he took the argument from her and carried it further:

'Maybe we should sell the television? Or give it away. Get
rid of it altogether. Especially with the children getting older.'

They watched each other for a few further seconds. At
length Rick rose, and wedged open the back door. Without a
word he unplugged the television set, carried it outside and
heaved it into the backseat of his car. A theatrical gesture,
perhaps — the disgraced television would sit there for several
days, tamely buckled in a rear seat-belt, before being traded in

for a new sound-system — but both felt somehow cleaner, even purified: a satisfaction akin to the sweet aftermath of spring-cleaning, or the riddance of vermin.

New routines quickly replaced the old. Their evenings were filled with music, with educational games — Scrabble, crosswords, Trivial Pursuit — and, above all, with books.

The young couple had inherited a reverence for books, both had brought several tea chests packed with books to the marriage: an intellectual dowry of children's books, old school texts, gift-sets of Shakespeare and Shaw and Jane Austen and assorted Brontës, plus, from Linda's side, everything that Dickens had ever written: a metre-length, at least, of matching volumes, bound in calf, plus assorted school paperback versions of the same titles. These had multiplied in the years since: each Christmas they received as gifts almost as many books as they gave. Their shelves — makeshift constructions of plank and brick — were crammed, *jammed;* unread books, many of them, but their presence alone was reassuring, their names were a kind of incantation, like the names of saints or household gods: small geometric household gods of learning and self-improvement and uplift; protectors against ignorance. The books had worn more sacred with time. They were dipped into, like the Bible, as sources of quotations, and poetry, and Trivial Pursuit clues — but seldom read.

Until now. Delivered from television, Linda decided they should read aloud to each other every night.

'As my father read to me,' she announced over a meal one evening, and immediately rose and began tugging books from the shelves before turning to invite Rick to help, or even to agree.

'Where shall we start?' she asked.

'Anywhere but Dickens,' he said, teasing her.

She smiled and squeezed the book she had already selected back into its narrow slot, and tugged out another.

At first there were frequent interruptions. Emma, placid from birth, slept unbroken from early evening to early morning, but her older brother insisted on staying awake with his parents. The television had often kept him tranquillised in the past; now new routines were needed. A war of attrition followed — a war of tears and nerve and bluff — ending in the parents' capitulation. Weary of running to the child's bedroom every few minutes, it simply seemed easier to have him with them, playing in the lounge, late at night. Listening to, or at least *hearing,* their book-readings also had a soothing, hypnotic effect on the child. His eyes drooped shut, his restless twitching ceased — often, oddly, at the end of a chapter, or on the last page of a book, as if cued by some subtle change in the tone of his mother's voice. Or was it some resolution in the music of the words themselves, words whose meanings were still largely beyond him?

'The growing good of the world,' his mother recited, *'is partly dependant on unhistoric acts; and that things are not so ill with you and me as they might have been, is half owing to the number who have lived faithfully a hidden life, and rest in unvisited tombs.'*

Rick — if he was still awake — would rise and carry the sleeping boy to bed at the end of such passages; this was the sign for a general lights-out.

Isolated from the wider world, their small, shared life contracted even more tightly about their children, their board-games and book-readings. Old friends from university, staff-room colleagues from school — many still single — were rarely seen. There seemed so little time. Linda had chosen to stay at home with Ben for the first year; Rick took leave without pay the next year while she went to work. The opposite pattern had continued with the birth of Emma. Rick had spent the year at home, mothering her; Linda went to school.

After that, they alternated work and home duties, but within their family geometry a further symmetry, or mirror-reflection, was growing: the father was closer to the daughter, the mother to the son.

3

Emma's sore throat seemed trivial at first: another of the shared communal viruses that were swapped back and forth between the toddlers at playgroup like counters, or dice, in a board-game. Made of tougher gristle than her older brother — less complaining, more robust — germs seemed to bounce off her. Rick and Linda paid little attention to her symptoms at first.

But the swollen glands remained swollen; a blood screen hinted at vague abnormalities.

Their local doctor — silver-haired, silver-tongued — was reassuring as he studied the print-out.

'I've seen numbers like this before,' he said. 'No cause for concern. Probably just a virus.'

'Could it be serious?'

He shook his head: 'Of course we'll repeat the test in a week or two. Just to make sure everything is back to normal.'

Rick and Linda exchanged glances: 'Then it *could* be serious?'

He smiled reassuringly, but the smile seemed to lack something: 'I can't see any point in worrying about it yet.'

They worried for a week: in small bursts at first, but lengthening, and growing, uncontrollably, as the child failed to improve.

The repeat screen was equally ambiguous. The doctor, while conceding the figures on his print-out 'might' not be as normal as he first thought, still refused to name any disease, or even nominate a short-list of candidates. He filibustered smoothly for some time before Linda interrupted:

'If it might be something, *what* might it be?'

'It would be premature to say. There are many possibilities.'

'Serious?'

'Some serious, some not so serious. But that applies to any illness ...'

This silver-haired man in a pin-stripe suit suddenly seemed less a doctor, than an actor playing a doctor. Rick and Linda rose simultaneously, angrily; Rick demanded a copy of both test print-outs, which were reluctantly provided. From a payphone in the waiting room they made an urgent call, and drove immediately to the rooms of a specialist paediatrician: Eve Harrison, an old school-friend of Linda. Short, compact, quick-talking, Eve had been known for her frankness at school; she showed no hesitation in applying a label to the blood screens at first glance, a word Rick and Linda had already begun to sense, if only from the glare of its previous absence.

Like most parents, they had rehearsed over the years for that moment, emotionally: the moment they might hear the word leukaemia spoken to *them,* spoken *at* them. They had grieved, vicariously, for other children: small strangers who were nevertheless part of the shared public property of parenthood. News of the illnesses of these others — friends of cousins of friends, or cousins of friends of cousins — spread as rapidly as jokes or gossip through a vast network of waiting, eaves-dropping parents, in hushed, horrified tones.

'How terrible — and such a lovely family.'

'Nothing can be done? Surely *these* days, with all the new drugs ...'

Beneath the horror of such stories there was also, surely, a deeper, half-hidden note of relief: that it wasn't happening to them, and theirs. Perhaps there was even an odd warped gratitude towards the victim, who had somehow — although this dark thought would never be put into words — saved everyone else by being chosen in their place: a statistical scapegoat, a statistical sacrifice.

For Rick and Linda there was also, at the end of that terrible week of worry, a kind of relief that it *had* happened to them, and theirs. Anything was better than uncertainty; the waiting had been intolerable, the fear of the unmentionable had almost come to be a desire for the unmentionable; its certainty, its *mention,* was at least a resolution. Finally to hear the word spoken aloud provided a focus for worry, a definite enemy that they could now face, and fight, together, as a family.

A bone marrow biopsy the following morning gave an even clearer view of this enemy.

'Remission is possible,' Eve Harrison told them, 'but everyone who has this type dies of it, eventually.'

The young parents glanced at each other, more composed and prepared: 'How long?'

'The mean survival rate is three years. Fifty per cent of the victims are still alive at three years.'

They felt almost grateful again for these blunt figures: three years was better than, well, three months. They felt, after the initial diagnosis had taken everything away, that they had been given something back.

Emma sat on the thick carpet in Eve's small office, solemnly reading a brightly coloured picturebook, ignoring their discussion. Three years was the length of her life to date: she was being offered her entire lifetime, repeated. Her parents sat watching her, breathing a little more easily. For the moment they could fall no further; they could even permit themselves a small ration of hope. A cure might well be found in three years. A marrow donor might even be found, although Eve was as frank as always on this: odd bloodlines in Rick's family — a Finnish great-grandparent — had left the child with a rare tissue-type, possibly unique.

'Of course we'll type you both,' she said. 'And Ben. And all the grandparents, if they're willing.'

'Of *course* they're willing.'

'You'd be surprised. Sometimes family members refuse.'

They were surprised, very surprised, but the issue was unimportant, and irrelevant to their overriding concern.

'I don't want to raise false hopes,' Eve said. 'I have to warn you that a match is very unlikely.'

4

Emma was a small, serious child: slow and methodical in her movements, a watcher of games rather than a participant.

'Wol,' Linda had nicknamed her, for her solemn owl-like appearance, wise beyond her years.

In the months that followed, her life revolved about the hospital. Giant scanners periodically engulfed and disgorged her; sharp needles pricked her tiny thumb-pads daily; drug combinations made her ill, or her hair fall out — but mostly it seemed a life of waiting, in bright primary-coloured ante-rooms filled with picturebooks and soft toys. Her parents often wondered what she made of it all, what exactly was going on behind those wide solemn owl-eyes. At the age of three her knowledge of death was limited. A pet goldfish had been buried in the backyard, under a small twig cross, with due ceremony, then promptly forgotten. Tears in her eyes, she had once chased away a neighbour's cat that was tormenting a spring fledgling on the back lawn. As if choosing to torment *her* instead, the cat had returned overnight and left a pair of tiny, stiff, inedible wings amid a scatter of soft down on the grass: a deliberate and malevolent gift, it seemed, for the little girl to find in the morning. Various species of squashed wildlife that lined the road to a beach holiday one summer had caused less misery — 'road pizza', Benjamin had called it, repeatedly, trying to shock his sister, but only making her giggle.

At four, during her first remission, there was a flurry of bedtime questions. *How old will you be when you die? Will you go to heaven, Mummy?*

The little girl had never appeared concerned by her illness while she was ill, but perhaps — her hair was growing back and she was gaining weight — she now half sensed that she was past it, and that it was safe to ask such questions. The subject of death would disappear within weeks, Eve Harrison

106

reassured the worried parents.

'It's just a phase, Linda. A normal, healthy phase.'

'But what do we *tell* her?'

'Tell her the truth. Tell her what you would like to hear in her place. These are normal four-year-old questions.'

Less normal was an awareness of her own mortality that emerged, obliquely, when signs of the disease returned the following year: a self-awareness that was bent, at first, into an obsession with the health of her grandparents, with the signs of age and deterioration of their bodies.

She burst into tears in the car, without warning, driving home, after a Sunday visit to Rick's parents.

'I don't want Grandma to die,' she blubbered.

Rick turned to face her, alarmed: 'She's not going to die, Wol, not for a long time. She's only fifty years old.'

'But her *hair* is so old.'

The child's own bald head — the scorched-earth of chemotherapy — was concealed by a bright, batik scarf. Linda, who was driving, stopped the car; Rick climbed out and into the backseat with Emma, Ben squeezed over the gear-shift into the front.

They drove on with the father nursing his daughter.

'No one is going to die, Wol,' he murmured. 'Not Grandma. Not anyone. Not for a long time. In our family everyone lives to be a hundred years old. *Every*one.'

But these were her own anxieties, self-anxieties, once removed; they could not be reasoned away.

'Are you going to be cremated or buried, Grandma?' she blurted across the dinner table the following Sunday.

Forewarned, fully briefed, the grandmother — a youthful

fifty-five — laughed lightly: 'It's so far away I haven't thought about it, Wol.'

The small girl watched her solemnly for a time.

'If you're cremated,' she finally said, 'you might not have a body to wear in heaven.'

The adults smiled at each other above her head, allowing themselves to be amused, *willing* themselves to be amused, but breathing a little more easily when Emma pushed herself away from the table and slipped off to play.

The deeper question — the blunt question they had all dreaded — took several more months to find its way through this maze of detours and displacements.

'Am I going to die, Mummy?'

Linda had woken around dawn to find Emma standing at the bedside, gazing down at her. Early birds twittered outside, the first light of morning sneaked between the curtain-chinks. She pulled aside the quilt, the little girl clambered up and in. Rick, waking more slowly, rolled to face them; the daughter lay nestled between her parents, her big owl-eyes glistening in the half-dark, gathering what little light there was. Her voice when she spoke was matter-of-fact, unafraid — having finally reached this destination she was far less concerned, it seemed, for herself, than she had been, months earlier, for the health of her grandmother.

'Will I go to heaven?'

'Of course. One day. Not for a long time.'

More questions followed: 'What will I do there? What will I do on my own? Who will look after me?'

She had clearly been preparing a list for some time.

'You won't be on your own, Wol. I'll already be there.

Grandma will already be there. We'll all be together.'

'What if I can't find you? What if I'm not allowed to see you?'

'Why wouldn't you find us?'

'Because I've been naughty.'

A catalogue of tiny misdemeanours followed; she was easily reassured that none was unforgivable. Having emptied herself, methodically, of these preoccupations, she fell asleep, leaving her parents facing each other, staring at each other in the half-dark, their warm breaths mingling, their thoughts desperately agitating.

5

'Worry achieves nothing,' Eve attempted to reassure the young parents. 'Worry is useless, a total waste of energy.'

There was nothing wasteful about Eve Harrison: her hair cropped short, her face free of make-up. Her clothes — plain smock, sensible, flat-heeled shoes — also seemed blunt, functional, to the point. Unadorned.

But the two parents increasingly wanted adornment, they wanted to hear reassuring fibs, or at least half-truths. Their need for bluntness had passed; they now wanted *cosmetics*. Despite Eve's advice, they had also come to depend on worry. Worrying was far from useless, they sensed: the worry process was a restless working-through of possibilities and permutations, an exhaustive examination of every path, every fork in the path. Rick, grown accustomed to insomnia over the years of Emma's illness, had come to think of those long hours of tossing and turning and worrying in bed as a search program: a brute-search, like a computer chess game he had bought as a birthday present to himself some years before. The game had obsessed him. He had glued himself to the video display, fascinated, every night for weeks, as the program checked the consequences of every possible move, counted possibilities, eliminated dead-ends in the maze of infinite possible end-games.

Worry was also a kind of fuel, he suspected: a higher-octane fuel, for a higher temperature furnace. It raised the metabolic rate, it provided the energy that kept them going, that was channelled into *doing* things, into actual physical tasks: the keeping of temperature charts, the counting of bruises, the frequent phone calls to Eve, the trips to the hospital. It got them through the day — through the mundane routine of each day. It also got them through the weeks, and months, and years, powering more optimistic, longer-range tasks: the correspondence that Rick began with tissue-banks and bone-marrow registers around the world, Linda's volunteer work with the Make-a-Wish Foundation and the Leukaemia Support Group.

At first resistant to these groups — unwilling to admit that Emma might ever come to need such wishes or support — she was dragged along to an Annual General Meeting by another parent, a mother she had met repeatedly in the same waiting rooms, and found herself nominated onto the support group's fund-raising committee. Soon she was immersed, finding a real satisfaction, almost a relief, in taking down the minutes, typing the monthly newsletter, xeroxing and mailing copies. She was, she felt, at last helping her child, playing her part, expending all that accumulated worry-energy usefully: a small cog in the wheel of Cure.

When the search for paths into the future ended in blind alleys, there was still the past to examine. The feeling was inescapable that they were somehow to blame, that it might even help if they *were* to blame. Had Linda taken some harmful drug during pregnancy? Drunk one glass too many of wine? Had there been something else in Emma's childhood environment? Something chemical or unnatural? Some toxin? If they could not blame themselves they blamed others. Linda's father — a heavy smoker, two packs a day — came under suspicion briefly.

'It's such a filthy habit, Dad,' Linda berated him one weekend, over a family meal. 'If you won't think of yourself think of others. I'm not saying it has anything to do with Wol, but who knows.'

Rick, unwilling to criticise his father-in-law directly, and specifically, told a more general story.

'I was at a curriculum meeting a few weeks ago. In at Head Office. There was only one smoker in the room. Jenny Adams — the chairperson — asked him to put out his cigarette. When he refused, she stood up, leaned across the table and, I kid you not, spat on him.'

His father-in-law was incredulous: 'She *what?*'

'She spat on him.'

'But that's disgusting.'

'Maybe. I don't say I agree with it, but I think we'll see more of it. If he pollutes her, she said, then she was going to pollute him.'

Linda's mother, quiet till that point, but seething with a growing anger, finally spoke up.

'I feel that *you* have spat on your father,' she said to Linda, and through Linda also to Rick. 'Here, tonight. You have spat on him in his own house. I don't like smoking any more than you, but to suggest it might have something to do with Wol — well, I think it's the most horrible thing you have ever said.'

Apologies followed, by phone, over several days; normal relations were gradually resumed. But despite Eve's reassurances, such obsessions consumed the next few years. Their older, gentler routines — nightly book-readings, weekend picnics — became episodic, haphazard. Even church attendance was disrupted. At first the boyish Reverend Cummings and his ancient congregation had been discreetly supportive as word of Emma's illness spread. Now, when the family did get to church, it was such an event, and such a fuss was made of Emma — so much consolation and pity and even, once, public prayers, were offered — that it became an ordeal.

'Never again,' Linda vowed, as they drove away one Sunday morning.

Rick defended the young priest: 'He didn't mention her by name.'

'But he was looking directly *at* her. How could he do that? Without even asking us?'

The children sat in the back seat, listening. They had heard the prayers, absorbed the sympathetic smiles of the congregation — there seemed little point in excluding them from the discussion.

'Aren't we going to church any more?' Ben asked.

'Not for a while.'

'But I want to go. Emma doesn't have to come if she doesn't want to, but I *want* to go.'

'We don't have time, Ben,' his father said firmly.

Always more difficult than his placid sister, the boy now demanded even more of their attention, as if to keep his share constant, or proportionate. At times he seemed almost jealous of his sister's disease. Over the years, he had been the sickly one, the designated patient, now he was forced to compete for space in the sickbed. Most mornings he complained of aches in the belly or chest or head. He frequently missed school, he insisted on accompanying the family to hospital, he demanded that Doctor Eve examine *his* ears or throat, listen to *his* chest.

On one memorable visit he even demanded that he, too, be given a needle.

Eve — grown tired of his pestering — was more than happy to oblige. She filled a syringe with saline solution and attached the largest-bore needle she could find. At the sight of that gleaming horse-needle, aimed in his direction, the boy changed his mind and fled the room, amid laughter.

6

At six, approaching the three-year survival milestone, the odds seemed to have altered in Emma's favour.

'To have come this far,' Rick asked Eve, or perhaps begged her, during their weekly visit, 'surely that gives her an even greater chance?'

Eve still had no time for false hope: 'It *might* mean she has even less. She has used up her allotted span.'

Her bluntness, which had once seemed an asset — if only because they knew she would never lie to them — on this

occasion seemed merely cruel. Rick shivered, a sudden invol-
untary spasm; Linda reached out and touched the polished
wood of Eve's desk.

Neither the protective magic of such gestures, nor the
prayers offered up in church, could ward off the greater power
of statistics, and the laws of probability. The disease returned a
few months later; 'active treatment' was stopped shortly
afterwards, after a last failure of response to chemotherapy. The
phrase, and its coy replacement — 'palliative treatment' —
seemed out-of-character for Eve Harrison: an evasion, which
in itself told the parents of the seriousness of Emma's plight.

'The effects of further treatment would be worse than the
disease,' she added, when pressed.

'There must be *something*.'

'We can offer transfusions if her blood count falls too low.
We can control bleeding, and infections ... But no more
chemotherapy.'

Eve glanced down at her desk, at a sheaf of blood-screens
that she had surely checked several times before: another
uncharacteristic avoidance.

'The time she has left isn't long,' she said. 'I see no point in
making her suffer unnecessarily.'

The parents held each other's gaze, waiting for the other to
act as spokesperson, waiting for one of their mouths to speak
the thought.

'*How* long?' Linda eventually, reluctantly, asked.

'A few weeks. Four. Six. It's difficult to be precise.'

Linda reached out her hand, Rick clasped it tightly.

'I promise that she will be comfortable,' Eve said. 'I promise
that she will feel no pain when the time comes. But that's all I
can promise.'

7

There was no time for hysterics, or further recriminations. Even tears seemed a luxury, an indulgence that had to be postponed.

Until.

One question had to be answered rationally, and immediately: how to spend those last few weeks together, how to make them at least halfway happy. The idea of a Last Wish trip to Disneyland or Disney World in America — or even to the cluster of smaller, closer Lands and Worlds on the Queensland Gold Coast — was repellent to both parents: bread and circuses.

What did you do afterwards, they asked each other? After closing time on the last day in Disneyland, pushing through the exit turnstiles in a queue of weary parents and overtired children? Surely that was a kind of death itself; and to pin happiness on one last wish was to die two deaths.

By the time they had argued this through — and changed their minds, and decided to override their squeamishness if it was Emma's wish — her weakness and fragility did not permit such long-distance trips.

Or so Eve Harrison told them. Eve was still their sole confidante; for the moment they decided to keep all four grandparents in the dark, or half-dark; avoiding constant visits, constant fussing. Above all, they sought normality, they sought to restore the family games, the music, the book-reading of an earlier, happier life. Perhaps they also half believed that a return to these routines might magically transport them back through time, or at least allow them to pretend that they were still back there, that the intervening horror had never occurred.

They also recalled the soothing, sedative effect those book-readings had on Ben: they were now in need of such sedation themselves.

'Where shall we start?' Linda asked her husband that first night, standing at the bookshelves, head tilted, reading the spines, after the two children had already been read to sleep.

'You had finished *Middlemarch*,' he said. 'You were working your way through Dickens.'

'It's so long ago I can't remember.'

'*I* remember,' he said, and they both managed a small laugh.

'You're not a fan?'

'I didn't like his last one,' he said, and they laughed again.

'Why don't you try *A Tale of Two Cities*?' he suggested.

She was surprised: 'You've read it?'

'I saw the film. A long time ago. I must have been eight or nine, but I remember it clearly.'

Head still tilted, she searched the close-packed shelves as he talked.

'My father took me,' he was saying. 'I was amazed — he never went to the movies. Sorry, the *pictures*. He always said they numbed the mind.'

'A man after my own heart.'

'Even more amazing — it was on a week night. We never went anywhere on week nights. And suddenly he arrived home from work and announced he was taking me to the pictures. Just me. It was an old film — black and white. I can't remember who was in it.'

'Charles Darnay and Sydney Carton.'

'The actors in the film?'

Linda laughed; she had been teasing him: 'The characters in the book.'

He wasn't listening to her; he was back in time, reliving that glowing night: 'I still remember the last scene. The hero climbs the steps, the guillotine waits. He makes a very moving speech — or maybe he only thinks the words. And suddenly he's lifted above it all — the guillotine, the basket of heads, the bloodthirsty mob, it's all a long way away, far *below* him. I had goosebumps all over. I must have been about Ben's age.'

'I wouldn't take Ben to it,' she said. 'Nine is too young. It would give him nightmares.'

'It's not really violent,' he said. 'Not by today's standards. And it meant a lot to me. I'd forgotten how much. Maybe I'll take him to the movies again when he's older.'

He paused: they both sensed that they were talking about a child with a future. Perhaps they were already talking about him as if he were an only child. They had broken an unspoken rule: that it was unfair to their daughter to make plans that did not include her, that were beyond her.

'I know what the book looks like,' Linda said, as she continued to search the shelves. 'It's not part of the set. Olive green binding, very old, a little tatty.'

At length she tugged the book from some deep recess, blew dust from the pages, then turned immediately to the last page, and began to read: *'It is a far, far better thing I do than I have ever done; it is a far, far better rest I go to than I have ever had.'*

They sat, silenced, sharing the same thought: that each would willingly, gladly, take the place of their small daughter in the tumbril. And yet they were powerless. They would have donated a kidney or lung to save her — they would have donated both lungs, they would each have sacrificed a still-beating *heart* — but their bone marrow, the only gift she needed, spread plentifully through their bodies, in far, far greater quantities than they would ever require themselves, was useless, even dangerous, to her.

8

In the following weeks Emma slowly became aware, again, of the existence of that tumbril in which she was riding, of the fact that it had turned a last corner, and the square ahead, and all it contained, had come into view. Had some developmental threshold been crossed in her growth? A spurt in the imagination, or brain-size, which permitted her to see the future clearly, or the absence of future, for the first time? Or had she come to sense, and be infected by, the desperation of her parents, which they always tried to shield from her? The attentions of her grandparents, fully briefed, finally, on the extent of her predicament, were a further cue. Her stoic, wise-owl manner vanished for longer intervals, and resisted jolting back to equilibrium. When she sat with her books, or paints, or drawing pads, her gaze was often fixed to one side, defocused.

Morbid fascination fuelled her talk at meal times: endless questions about bones, dust, ashes, cremation, coffins. She solemnly examined the blue-black bruises that appeared on her body, at times even measured those bruises with her school ruler in a parody of her parents' earlier obsession.

As the end also became clearer to Rick and Linda, they resumed church-going, choosing to look pity in the eye, to stare it down, to spurn it. In part this return to the fold was still a search for the routines of normality, an attempt to travel backwards in time; in part it was a last desperate reaching out — not for miracles, perhaps, but at least for answers. Each Sunday at St Paul's they huddled together in a back pew, in a far corner, wanting only a private, family worship, a communion between them and whichever God might haunt the old church. Privacy was not so easy: once again the Reverend Cummings insisted on intervening, mediating — translating — between them and that God. He asked for shared prayers from the congregation, mentioned their trials in sermons; and after Rick protested, politely but firmly, began visiting them at home instead, uninvited.

'Don't forget the power of faith,' he exhorted over innumerable cups of tea. 'The power of prayer.'

Linda had reached exasperation point.

'I don't understand,' she said, 'why that would help. And if it did, what kind of God would insist on it? Why should we have to *beg* for favours?'

He sat back in an armchair — Rick's leather armchair, appropriated — and pursed his lips and pressed his fingertips together. Like the family doctor, years before, he seemed to his hosts to be enacting a role, playing a part meant for someone older: a wise uncle, or grandfather.

'I don't want to sound glib,' he murmured, 'but if we knew all the answers — if knowledge was given to us on a plate — what would be the point of faith?'

'That's fine advice for us,' she said. 'But what do we tell *her*? Jesus wants her for a sunbeam?'

'Perhaps she doesn't want to be told anything,' he said. 'In many ways this is a far more difficult test for you.'

'What are you saying? This is a *test*? This was given to us as a test of faith? What's the answer? Is it an essay, or multiple choice?'

He paused before answering, shocked by her harshness. He licked his lips, his mouth opened and closed without speaking, groping for an answer that was not quite ready. He was out of his depth. His avuncular manner had vanished, his eyes reddened, he was close to tears.

'Remember the story of Abraham and Isaac?' he finally said, huskily. 'The Lord tested Abraham's faith by asking him to sacrifice his son.'

Despite his anguish, Linda's face instantly purpled with rage.

'Fuck you,' she said. 'And fuck any God who would play such horrible games.'

Rick rose from his chair, unastonished by the words she had spoken, even though he had never heard her utter such words before, or even seen such an extreme of anger. The same feelings, if not the same words, were on the tip of his own tongue; there was nothing else that could be felt.

'Perhaps I didn't choose my example well. What I meant to say ...'

'I think we've talked enough, Bill,' Rick said. 'We'd like to be alone.'

As they stood at the door, holding each other, watching the Reverend Cummings drive away for the last time, they realised suddenly how much they had aged in the past months, at a much faster rate than their household clocks and calendars had measured out. It seemed that this young priest, approximately their own age, now belonged to a still younger generation. His were the words of someone with little experience of life — or, surprisingly, given his office, of death, or at least of the death of the young; his advice still came from books, or manuals.

'It's up to us,' Rick said to his wife. 'No one can help except us.'

9

The priest's words of advice stuck fast in their minds nevertheless, like a tune heard once in the morning that can't be shaken off, repeating, interminably, through the day. The possibility that it *was* somehow a test, an ordeal, a trial, was difficult to shake loose, if only because of its deeper implication: that therefore there must also be a solution. Their powerlessness was deformed into guilt, which was bent itself into overattentiveness, into a smothery kind of love that the little girl was forced sometimes to turn away from, to *hide* from. Famine-thin, increasingly fragile, easily bruised, it was as if she sensed that her parents might cuddle her to death, or at least cuddle her back into hospital. She shut herself in her room for long periods, alone, and — it seemed to Rick and Linda, in their worst moments — betrayed.

'It's as if there's a wall there. We're on one side, she's on the other.'

'We can't help her, but I think she thinks we *won't* help her.'

The worry-program had bypassed one possible solution, or pathway, much earlier, but goaded by guilt, and self-blame, returned to it, was dragged back to it, again and again — although for some time neither discussed the path with the other, believing that for the first time in their marriage their thoughts had diverged too widely, that the idea was so outrageous, so *unspeakable,* that no two sane people would ever think it together.

Rick first spoke the unspeakable. They lay talking in bed in the small hours, trying, as always, to talk each other to sleep, to talk themselves empty, to talk out the day's accumulated worries.

'Maybe we should all go together,' he said, inserting the words suddenly, without warning, into a lull in a conversation about household finances.

'What do you mean?'

'Just that. We shouldn't let her go ... alone.'

'You mean ... we should go *with* her?'

Linda's tone was surprisingly calm; he peered at her through the half-dark, trying to read her face.

'You don't seem surprised,' he murmured.

'It crossed my mind too. I've thought of it several times. I've tried *not* to think it — it seemed too crazy.'

She shivered in his arms: a convulsion that was more a shudder of disgust. He shivered himself, contagiously.

'It *is* crazy,' he told her. 'It's crazy even to talk about it.'

She rolled away from him, but he followed, pressing against her from behind: 'There's Ben to think of, if nothing else,' she said. 'What right would we have to take him with us?'

Even now the idea was only half speakable, couched in the euphemisms of travel and journeys. Of family holidays.

'He would hate to be left out,' Rick said, and they both suddenly laughed, briefly, too-loudly, then lay together for some minutes in silence, their bodies stilled, their hearts pounding, not quite believing that such thoughts had crept out into the open, and were being discussed.

The subject of Ben had opened another door, forced the worry-program to throw up another weird solution, only slightly less unspeakable. This time it was Linda who found the words:

'Maybe only one of us should go with her. Maybe I should go with her.'

Rick rolled apart from her: 'You want me to lose *both* of you?'

'Is your grief going to be *worse*?' she said. 'Could it *be* any worse?'

'Of course it would be worse.'

She could hear the doubt in his voice; she knew that he was already there, ahead, or at least abreast of her.

She spoke, as of old, for them both: 'Are two griefs worse than one? How much worse can it be? Can things be worse than *worst*?'

Their hearts pounded on as they lay there at rest, in bed. Sweat broke out across Rick's face, his hands shook, the sheets were damp and clammy against his skin. The darkness, crowding and claustrophobic, surrounded him; it seemed a viscous element, heavy on his senses, preventing clear thought.

'This is absurd,' he said. 'We'll have other children. We can have another baby straight away.'

'It's not us we're talking about,' Linda said.

He lay in silence, rebuked.

'It's Wol,' she continued. 'I can't bear to think of her going away — alone. It's as though we've cast her out into the woods. Abandoned her, like something in a fairytale. And we won't go with her.'

She paused; the idea was growing, taking more definite shape: 'I *want* to go with her,' she announced, more definitely.

'I don't want to hear any more about it,' Rick said. 'It's late. We're both exhausted. In the clear light of day you'll realise how crazy this is.'

'Just think about it,' she urged. 'That's all I ask.'

He rolled away from her, to the far side of the bed.

'No,' he said, angrily, 'I won't. Not ever. I don't want to hear about it again.'

10

As the child's immune system failed, she was fed an exotic salad of antibiotics to prevent infection; these in turn suppressed her appetite, she lost weight steadily over the last weeks. She rapidly came to resemble the snapshots of her forgotten foster siblings in Bangladesh and Ecuador: all skin and bones, her eyes sunk deeply into their dark sockets. Her period of self-isolation had passed, she now preferred to sleep in her parent's bed each night, between them, facing her father — which meant that they often didn't sleep themselves, anxious not to squash her frail bird-bones or bruise her thin flesh. Often Linda would leave father and daughter together, sneaking off into Emma's room, or into Ben's room, spending the night squeezed even more uncomfortably into the narrow bed of a boy who was as unwilling as ever to be left out.

And as Rick lay there, sleepless, his daughter's small milky breath puffing rhythmically into his face, the realisation grew: that if their lunatic plan was ever followed through, if someone *did* choose to go with her, of course it would be him, not

Linda. The child would want him with her, his presence would most reassure her.

He decided, for the moment, to keep this realisation to himself.

Eve Harrison was visiting the house daily at the time, checking Emma's temperature, listening to her chest, peering into orifices. And pricking her thumb-pads, siphoning tiny drops of blood for analysis.

'Does she have to go through this?' Linda asked, but the needles seemed to bother her more than her stoical daughter.

Several times Eve urged hospitalisation, but both parents had decided that Emma would die — although they still couldn't bring themselves to utter the blunt word — at home, in a familiar world, believing it would be her own wish.

Home had one other advantage, unspoken: although no decision had yet been made, and their lunatic plan had not been discussed again, both knew that it would be impossible to carry out in hospital.

'How can hospital help her?' Linda demanded of her friend.

'She may need a transfusion. Depending on the blood count.'

'Couldn't she be transfused at home?'

Eve was reluctant to agree, but it was the reluctance of fixed habits: 'I suppose I could arrange a home-care nurse,' she conceded.

This was not enough for Linda: 'I can do whatever needs to be done — I'm sure I can. With your help, of course.'

'It's a twenty-four-hour job. When will you sleep? She will need constant nursing attention.'

'We'll work in shifts. I'll sleep when Rick is awake.'

'A night-nurse, then. Someone who'll watch her overnight. Please, you can't do it all yourself.'

Rick, listening to the debate, intervened: 'We don't want to share the remaining time with strangers, Eve. Surely you can understand that?'

Eve, ever practical, quickly realised that to argue with these stubborn parents was a waste of time. A crash course in basic nursing procedures followed, under her supervision. True to her promise, she left a stash of pain-killing liquids and suppositories, and several syringes and ampoules of stronger stuff, with written instructions on dosage schedules. An impromptu lecture on the properties and uses of each drug was followed by a kind of brief oral exam, or viva — delivered with Eve's characteristic efficiency. This in turn was followed by a practical tutorial: she arrived one morning with a bag of big navel oranges and had her two mature-age students slipping small butterfly needles through the skin of the fruit, getting the 'feel'.

'There should be no need for these,' Eve said. 'But just in case. If she bleeds, I can instruct you by phone on what to give.'

Having passed the orange-test, they moved on to human flesh: jabbing needles into each other's veins, repeatedly, under Eve's scrutiny. There was an odd relief in this, a mix of slapstick comedy and pain, which provided, temporarily, a release from their preoccupations.

'Stick to the dose I've suggested,' Eve advised, leaving. 'These are powerful drugs. Too much could be fatal.'

Rick wondered for a moment if she were suggesting the exact opposite, subtly: offering them a final pain-relief for

Emma — a final safety net. Although of course Eve had no inkling of the full extent of their hidden agenda.

An agenda that was still half-hidden, also, from each other. Their minds were moving in parallel: along true parallel lines, never touching. Rick, especially, refused to admit that he was still giving the matter thought. At times the plan seemed outrageously stupid — even the simple sums were so wrong. At other times it seemed inevitable, logical — even if it was the logic of despair.

Finally, discussion could be deferred no more: an oblique mention by Linda began a series of escalating arguments. Soon they were debating, whispering heatedly, each night in bed, and thinking up counter-arguments in silence all day, with Ben at school, but Emma, too fragile now for school, hovering at brink of ear-shot. At first these discussions were in subjunctive mode, preceded by an 'if' or a 'should'; this kept the unspeakable hypothetical, and permitted a discussion of the plan — The Plan — as if it were science-fiction, or a kind of algebra which did not deal with real events and things yet still allowed a plan of action to be fleshed out, and modified, and tested.

'*If* we told her,' Linda said, 'that you were going with her, then we could never change our minds. We could never take it back. We would have to be absolutely certain before we could tell her.'

Behind these abstractions there was a mounting urgency, for time was short. Emma, too, appeared to sense this. She began sleeping poorly; refusing to go to bed, to any bed, even to her parents' bed. She actively resisted sleep. Rick and Linda would wake at night to hear her padding about the house, or softly singing songs in the dark bed between them. Once they were woken by the dazzle of the bedside lamp to find her propped up between them in bed, reading.

'I don't feel tired,' she explained.

When pressed to turn out the light and shut her eyes, she burst into tears: 'What if I don't wake up?'

'One day, Wol,' Rick told her, 'you will wake up and you will be in heaven. You will close your eyes, here on earth, and when you open them you will be somewhere else.'

They lay together in bed, the small girl cuddled between her parents. The emotion of the moment stripped bare the clichés he was speaking, freed them from trite associations. They were, simply, the only words that could be uttered.

Rick's heart pounded, he prepared himself to speak again, to force out the next words, knowing that once they were spoken they were a promise, binding and irrevocable. As he opened his mouth, Linda suddenly reached over and gripped his arm.

'Don't,' she said. 'Please. We need more time to think it through.'

11

From that night on every light in the house was left burning — even, or especially, Ben's bedroom light, where he demanded equal treatment. But Emma's fear of the dark, also, flushed her parents' discussions out into the open, into the light, from behind the cover of hypothetical ifs and shoulds.

'We need counselling,' Linda suggested. 'That we could even *contemplate* it, don't you think we're a bit mad? That we need some sort of help?'

'No,' he said. 'I mean — yes, maybe we are mad. But no — no counselling. They'd take her away from us. They'd take them *both* from us.'

'But we've lost perspective. We're irrational. So caught up in this we can't see the wood for the trees.'

'Maybe that's the best perspective.'

To some extent the two sides of these debates were interchangeable: pro and con arguments were rotated between them. The deeper disagreement was not between the two parents, but within each of them.

'It's such a weight,' Linda said. 'If we could at least talk it over with someone. With friends.'

'Which friends? Who could we possibly burden with this? I wouldn't wish it on my worst enemy.'

In this fashion, passed back and forth, a shared load, too hot or too heavy to handle alone, it was slowly decided. When their daughter next burst into tears, and refused to risk sleep, and Rick opened his mouth, Linda held her peace, allowing him to speak.

The words still took some time to emerge, they seemed stuck to the dry roof of his mouth.

'When you die, Wol,' he said, 'whenever it is, I will be there with you. I am going to die before you.'

Her tears had vanished; she watched him, curious.

'How do you know that?'

'I can make myself die,' he told her. 'With an injection. I'm going to die first, so I'll be there waiting for you.'

Also so there could be no turning back, no chickening out, abandoning her after she had died. This also had been planned — that she was to see him dead, to *know* him dead, before she died herself.

A calm gravity returned to her face. She asked a few further questions — technical questions — then within minutes her wide Wol-eyes closed, and she was sleeping, snuggled against her father's still-pounding heart. He realised that she took it for granted that he would choose to die with her; it was a wonderful comfort, yes, but his intended sacrifice — a sacrifice of everything — meant nothing else to her. He saw no selfishness in her reaction, not even the normal self-centredness of a child, but an entirely reasonable interpretation of events to an intelligent six-year-old mind: if heaven was such a wonderful place, why wouldn't he choose to come with her?

His own view of the road ahead was a little more terrifying. And yet — at the same time, once the decision had been made and was locked in place — oddly exciting. A far, far better place? He doubted it. Whatever faith he had once had now seemed shallow: a routine, social faith. He felt he was going nowhere, just ending — but perhaps those last few days, and especially nights, of peace, would make it worthwhile. And perhaps, just *perhaps* ...

'You know the cemetery's a bit like home to me,' he whispered to his wife, in bed.

She set aside the book she was reading and looked at him, disturbed, uncertain of his tone: 'Rick, don't be morbid.'

'No, I've been there before. As a boy. I once spent a Saturday night in the local graveyard, camping with a friend.'

She listened, reluctantly. Once such a story would have surprised her, now it seemed little more than tame; she knew that both of them had depths that were darker and weirder than had once seemed possible.

'It was his idea,' Rick was saying. 'My friend's. We each told our parents we were staying at the other's. We took our sleeping bags, and lay there most of the night, among the gravestones, telling ghost stories, trying to terrify ourselves.'

She shivered: 'You must have been crazy.'

'It was a dare — you had to do it. But it was an anticlimax. Suddenly it was morning — we must have slept — and nothing had happened. Of course we were heroes at school, we made up all kinds of horror stories. But deep down I was disappointed. It was the end of something, the end of the tooth-fairy. There just wasn't anything out there, no other dimension. There were no ghosts.'

12

Ben was told of the plan — after further intense discussion — the following night. Both parents were unsure what he would make of it, had even worried that he might demand to go too, jealous to the end of the way his entire world had come to orbit another, different focal point: his younger sister.

To him, their explanation was subjunctive again, peppered with ifs and maybes and even with the outright lie that the decision was not yet made, and what did he, Ben, think?

The boy moved to his mother's side, for once silent and undemanding, and held tightly to her, and watched his father for some time, unable to grasp fully what was being said to him, but sensing its gravity. Rick prattled on, talking far too quickly, telling his son that one day they would be together again, all of them, that until then he would have to look after his mother, that he would be the man of the house.

The boy stared at him, uncomprehending — perhaps, even

at nine, disbelieving. Explanations that had sounded profound the night before — talk of journeys, of waking in heaven, of future meetings — now sounded banal, or untrue, or even meaningless. Not for the first time, panic overwhelmed Rick, a wave of terror of the enormity, and absurdity, of the scheme. For the first time also — as his son watched him, suspiciously — he wondered also at the long-term effects it would surely have on the boy. Agitated, emptied of words, he left the child with Linda, and swallowed a sleeping pill that Eve had prescribed for both of them some months before. He knew that he wouldn't sleep, but at least he might be calmed. Later, in the silence of the very smallest hours, as the rest of the household slept, he rose from his bed, and spent much of the night writing a series of letters to his son: letters to be opened yearly, posthumously, on each successive birthday. He began with simple declarations of love — messages to a little boy from his father in heaven — then for the later years a gradually more complex mix of explanations and exhortations, and, finally, requests for forgiveness. He tried to recall his own states of mind, his own level of development, at various ages — ten, thirteen, sixteen — and tailor his messages accordingly. This was not as difficult as it first seemed: the chronology of the letters, splashed here and there with tears, followed, simply, the evolving complexity of his own thoughts as the long night progressed. The earlier letters to a younger Ben were drafts for the more subtle and sophisticated versions that the boy would open as he grew older.

You are 18, it's been a year since we last talked, and this is the last time we will talk. I hope these letters have not been a burden to you — hauntings from an old ghost. You are nearly as old as I am now, writing this, and it would seem presumptuous to offer any more guidance ...

Some time before dawn he heard Linda rise and begin moving about in the kitchen. He finished the last letter, and joined her outside on the back terrace. She was sitting at the garden table with a pot of coffee and two cups, clearly expecting him.

He seemed to have spent all his agitation of the night before; extruded it, poured it into that pile of letters. The outside world was starkly defined: sharp silhouettes and edges, a world of knife-edge clarity. An early bird glided between trees in a neighbour's backyard; the cool air was so still that Rick imagined he could feel the trace of the bird's passage: a faint stirring of wings, a spreading ripple.

Perhaps the tranquillity of the morning seduced them, lulled them both into the belief that their plan was not as difficult or as stupid as it had often seemed. Sitting there, holding hands, sipping coffee as light slowly flooded the eastern sky, they decided, almost matter-of-factly, as if scribbling a dental appointment in a diary, on the date.

13

On the second-to-last evening the four grandparents were invited to dinner. They arrived bearing gifts: big soft toys, chocolates for the children. There were no gifts for Rick; he watched, wistfully, as his parents and parents-in-law spent the evening fussing over Ben and Emma, careful to share their attentions, and their gifts, equitably. There was no way of telling them what was planned, or receiving his due share of that attention. There was no proper way of saying goodbye.

Linda brought her father an ashtray as they sat in the family room, sipping pre-dinner drinks, but he declared that he had given up.

'Weeks ago,' his wife added, mildly. 'It's the one good thing to come out of all this.'

The evening ended with offers from both grandmothers to stay in the house 'until the end' — offers that were politely, even gratefully, declined. On the doorstep Rick hugged his mother, and then, impulsively, his father. The older man, surprised to receive any sign of affection beyond the usual handshake, hugged him back.

'Be strong,' he said. 'Our thoughts are with you.'

On the last evening the smaller family ate together at the nearby Pizza Hut, a favourite of the children. Unwilling to carry Emma, increasingly frail, past a hundred staring faces, Rick had rung the manager; they were permitted to arrive and eat early, half an hour before opening time. At home afterwards the four of them played Monopoly — both children as engrossed as always, both parents unable to concentrate. Rick rose and swallowed another sleeping pill; then, sitting at his desk, listening to Mozart, he finished a long letter to his parents, asking for forgiveness, hoping for understanding. He also tore open the last letter he had written to Ben, to be read on his eighteenth birthday, and added several more words of love. Perhaps it was the Mozart, perhaps it was the sedative leaching into his veins, but with these tasks completed he found himself facing events, if not with equanimity, then at least once again with certainty.

Linda appeared in the door, agitated, trembling: 'We can't go through with this. It's absurd.'

He led her into the bedroom, they lay down together on the bed and held each other tightly. They had planned to make love one last time, but the act suddenly seemed irrelevant, and meaningless. She was still trembling; he rose and fossicked a Bible from the bookshelves, and for a time they read alternately: the poetry of Isaiah, Paul's letters to the Corinthians, St Matthew's version of the Sermon on the Mount, various Psalms. The texts held only a minimal promise for Rick — 'we'll see,' he joked grimly to himself — but some deeper music in the words had a soothing effect on both of them, like the drug he had swallowed, or the Mozart itself: *Yea, though I walk through the valley of the shadow of death, I will fear no evil: for thou art with me ...*

It seemed the culmination of all their nights of book-readings, as if those thick books — Dickens, George Eliot, Thackeray — had been a preparation for this moment, this last distillation of the written word.

In the next room someone landed on Mayfair, with hotels; the children abandoned their game and joined them in bed. Linda slipped a small butterfly-needle into Rick's veins, and taped it in place, despite shaking hands; she then repeated the procedure on Emma, finding the task surprisingly easy: the girl's veins were more prominent than her father's, her skin far more delicate than any thick-skinned navel orange. Emma flinched, momentarily, then watched as two syringes were loaded with morphine. Her wide owl-eyes seemed to be looking at everything simultaneously, taking everything in.

They lay together on the bed, all four of them — just as they had been together at Emma's birth, six years earlier, in the Maternity Suite at the local hospital. Ben seemed finally to grasp the enormity of what was planned, his eyes had reddened, but the seriousness, the methodical ritual of events, seemed to keep any terror in check. They had debated allowing him to watch, to participate, but even now, at the point of no return, there was surely something less terrifying, and certainly less bloody, about this occasion for him than there had been at his sister's birth, when her strange alien-being seemed to burst from his mother's innards. Linda felt that for his peace of mind later, as an adult, he should be a participant; he should *be* there. He listened quietly as they explained the last few steps, he kissed his father, and lay on top of him.

And so they lay together, a last few minutes of hand-holding, and tears, before separating. Emma seemed less concerned than her brother. Her clear contentment, lying there, clutching her father's hand, forced the last doubts from Rick's mind, and induced a parallel contentment in him. His heart pounded, but the flow of his thoughts was suddenly calm and steady. Even Linda felt that her daughter's serenity somehow cancelled out, at least for the moment, whatever misery she and her surviving child would subsequently endure.

When her husband was ready, she nodded, and pressed her face softly onto his, and he squeezed his own syringe, and waited, holding them all, but not for any length of time.

The List of All
ANSWERS

1

Again the child plucked at his mother's sleeve.

'Why do onions make my eyes water?' he demanded to know. 'Why?'

She shook her arm free and continued chopping the slippery, soapish segments, trying to ignore him. But there was no escape.

'Mummy, Mummy, why do ...?'

At precisely that moment the idea first came to her.

'Three,' she said.

'Three?'

'Three,' she repeated, not exactly sure what she meant herself. 'The answer to your question is — three.'

Silence descended while the child puzzled at this.

'What's three mean?' he shortly came out with.

His father, slicing tomatoes at the other end of the bench, intervened: 'One of Mummy's little jokes. *Another* of Mummy's little jokes.'

He glanced severely at his wife, she smiled steadily back. How else was she to cope? Battling away in a classroom full of year fives all day, then home to this. A second classroom, she was beginning to think it. No, worse: a second front.

'The head is like a pressure-cooker,' she began to explain, speaking in the direction of her son, but actually through him to his father. 'It can only hold so much.'

She paused, and glanced at her husband. He sliced a tomato clinically, pretending to ignore her. She turned back to the boy: 'If a joke doesn't emerge from the mouth, steam will shoot out the ears ...'

'Or worse,' the husband added, also talking through the medium of their child.

'I still don't get it,' the boy said. 'What's number three?'

She still didn't get it herself completely: a half-formed notion, the tip of a berg she could barely sense beneath the surface.

'Number three,' she told him, 'on the list.'

'What list?'

'I'll show you after dinner.'

'What's for dinner?'

She bit her tongue. These endless chains of question and response — once begun there was no ending them. From the moment she collected the child from the creche to the moment he finally succumbed to sleep some hours later — his chatter ceasing suddenly, his neck muscles giving out, head plopping softly onto the pillow mid-sentence — he never stopped plucking sleeves, turning up that insistent face, repeating his endless interrogations. *Why, Mummy? Why?*

'The list,' he remembered as he helped the two of them clear the table after dinner. 'The list! The list!'

'Yes, the list,' his father echoed, teasing, but with a harder edge to his voice. 'Show us the list.'

She retreated to the study and tucked a sheet of quarto into the typewriter. The list took some time to emerge, it was little more than an idea, after all. A vague shape. As for her typing — search and destroy, her husband liked to mock it.

The List Of All Possible Answers, she typed across the top of the page, patiently seeking out each key, and destroying. That accomplished, she moved down the page in a vertical column.

#1: No.

#2: Maybe.

139

#3 ...

Here she paused. Three? She was tired, the thoughts refused to flow ... *Because,* she finally improvised, then tugged her handiwork from the carriage and returned to the kitchen.

As she taped the list to the fridge door, her husband peered over her shoulder.

'"Because",' he muttered. 'What kind of answer is that? "Because" what?'

'"Because" nothing. Just "because".'

'Sounds like a cop-out to me.'

'It's not a definitive list,' she defended herself. 'Feel free to add to it.'

He opened the fridge door and unzipped a can of beer.

'Because that's the way God made it,' he suggested, sipping. 'Because that's the way God meant it to be.'

She laughed out loud: 'Who was accusing whom of a cop-out?'

She yanked open the kitchen oddments drawer, scrabbled among the odds and ends, and emerged with a pen. *Because that's the way things are,* she added to the list, landing the full-stop with an audible thump.

'It's still a cop-out,' he insisted. 'You want a beer?'

'Four,' she said.

'You want *four* beers?'

She shook her head: 'The answer to your question is four.'

He glanced again at the list.

'I don't see any number four.'

She yawned: 'Ask me tomorrow. I'm going to bed.'

2

She watched with interest as he plucked his first can from the fridge the next evening after work.

#4: he read. *Ask me again tomorrow.*

'Your list of all answers,' he told her, 'is beginning to look like a list of all evasions.'

'Congratulations,' she said. 'You just caught on.'

The list grew quickly in the days that followed. *#5: What Do You Think?* was pencilled in the following night, and *#6: Because I said so* added the night after that. Towards the end of the week, however, the rate in increase seemed to slow. After *#7: You're too young to understand* there were no further additions for several days.

'Finished, have we?' her husband, who had been pretending to ignore it all, couldn't prevent himself from asking. 'Finished our little list?'

'No,' she said.

'How many more?'

She paused, considering.

'A finite number,' she guessed. 'Maybe ten.' She paused, pleased with the roundness, the rightness of the figure. 'Yes, ten should just about cover everything.'

'What's "finite" mean, Mummy?'

Her husband's gaze caught hers; he waited, challenging. She thought for a moment, then reached for her pen:

#8: she wrote. *Look it up in the Britannica.*

She smiled back at her husband, smugly: 'Maybe not even ten. Maybe eight will cover everything.'

For a time it seemed that she was right. For several days she successfully deflected the child's questions, glancing up from lesson preparations, or from housework, to snap *Three* or *Seven* or *Four* — and especially, repeatedly, *One*.

The child kept pressing, as if trying to test the limits of the list, to push beyond, break its shackles. His questions seemed to become more difficult to field, more abstract. In church the following Sunday he finally seemed to find the theme he had been looking for: some garbled naive version of things he had heard in the sermon, or overheard as he scribbled in his colouring book, and which he began to hark on as soon as the benediction was over.

'Where is heaven, Mummy? Were we in heaven before we were born?'

They walked home in dazzling sunshine, holding hands: two parents with their small child between them, all in Sunday-best. The rituals of church, the singing, the drone of prayers, usually soothed her at the end of a hard school week, but not today. She could sense her husband waiting for her answers, ready to pounce.

'Shall we stop at the playground?' she suggested.

'Is Grandma in heaven? Will you go to heaven? Will we see God in heaven?'

'The answer to that could be nine,' her husband intervened — aid from an unexpected quarter.

'Nine?' the child wondered.

'Ask Mummy when she's in a better mood,' he said. 'Ask Mummy when she's learnt a little patience.'

They turned in at their gate, and entered the house. He

took a red felt-tip pen from the oddments drawer and added the words in inch-high letters at the bottom of the list. *#9: ASK MUMMY WHEN SHE'S IN A BETTER MOOD.*

'Enough is enough,' he said. 'The joke has gone too far.'

3

The blank facade of the fridge struck him the moment he entered the kitchen the following night. Once again, she was watching carefully.

'Where's the list?' he asked.

'Where's the list?' their child, trotting behind, echoed.

'You were right,' she said. 'The list had gone too far.'

Her husband smiled, relieved, but the child's lower lip began to tremble.

'I want my list,' he stammered. 'I want my answer list.'

His father bent to comfort him: 'The list has gone. It was a silly list.'

The child would not be comforted. 'No,' he shouted, twisting away. 'No! I want my list.'

As he ran from the room, his mother was already sifting through the kitchen wastebasket. She found the crumpled sheet, smoothed it between hand and bench, and began to tape it back onto the fridge.

'Please,' her husband said. 'No.'

'Yes,' she insisted.

'How much longer?'

'I don't know,' she admitted. 'I honestly don't know.'

He took a pen from his pocket.

#10: he wrote. *I don't know. I honestly don't know.*

He ruled a thick line across the page beneath his words. If nothing else, there would, surely, be no need for further entries.

What Comes
NEXT?

There is nothing as empty as the future,
or as bleached and pale blue: a type of summer,
a long school holiday, unpunctuated even
by our little lives, rounded with brackets.

Outside those brackets, what? Or — far worse — why?
Don't ask so many questions, wise adults
repeated, often, when I was young —
but each year I push an extra candle

through the crust and panic:
another pilot-flame to extinguish, quickly,
lest something uncontrollable ignites,
or I find myself breaking through icing

into the molten stuff beneath, suddenly
reduced to composite materials.
Perhaps this is the final homecoming:
a fair and even redistribution of matter;

my atoms permitted to cease their restless
jiggling, at peace among the other particles;
my bits and pieces returned to where
I sprang from — or less I, than me;

and less me, than him: his handful of carbon
returned to that topsoil, his water-quota — fifty litres —
to those streams and clouds, his ash to that ash;
his dust to *that* dust, there, no longer mine.